WELCOME TO
SOMERVILLE GRANGE

DONALD MONTGOMERY

ONE
WELCOME TO SOMERVILLE GRANGE

If we are to believe the effusive claims in the expensively produced brochure, Somerville Grange, must surely be paradise on earth, an oasis of contentment, free from the stress and squalor of the outside world. A haven for the fortunate few who have struggled valiantly throughout their lives and, one way or another, find themselves with the wherewithal to meet the extortionate cost of passing their remaining days in such sublime circumstances.

Nor are the claims excessive. Somerville Grange is situated in a sheltered valley, surrounded by verdant hills folded round an old Georgian manor house. A modest Palladian pile, happily rescued from decay by an astute member of a family which once aspired to great things and who would surely be impressed by the entrepreneurial spirit shown by the present incumbent.

Having inherited not only the crumbling manor house, but also fifty acres of scenic grounds, the central feature being an ornamental lake, Simon Forsyth, the new lord of the manor as it were, risked ridicule from timid brethren and plunged immediately into his great project. Even as the original house was being restored, building work was underway to construct what would eventually become a mixed colony amid this idyllic setting, comprising no less than two hundred and thirty dwellings; bungalows, cottages and villas and attractive terraces of smaller but only marginally less expensive flats.

There was never any doubt in Simon Forsyth's mind that Somerville Grange would be anything other than a retirement village, but crucially it would be the Rolls Royce of retirement communities. He was happy to make his own home in one of the impressive villas with unrestricted views across the lake, looking over the immaculate lawns beyond, fringed by tidy borders of spruce, birch and sturdy oak. This allowed the main building, the original Grange, to be developed into a community centre par excellence.

From the outset, Simon intended Somerville Grange to be more than just a retirement home; he wanted it to be a lively vibrant community. The ballroom of the old house, which had once aspired to splendour, was converted into a rather grand village hall. This has become the venue for communal activities of all kinds; resident association meetings, whist drives and sedate afternoon tea dances. It is used by the enthusiasts in the am-dram club to stage their idiosyncratic productions and has even hosted the odd wedding reception, when, somewhat late in the day, Cupid has come calling among the aged and aging residents.

In the thirty-odd years since the first affluent retirees moved in, Somerville Grange has achieved acclaim as the ultimate – or perhaps, strictly speaking, one should say the penultimate – heavenly destination for its fortunate residents.

Over the years, the Grange has been host to a variety of individuals, each for a fleeting moment making their mark in the enclosed community. In the early days, a robust ex-army type made the national press on account of his elaborate moustaches, a trivial nine-day wonder but a boon for Simon Forsyth's marketing department.

More recently, Moira Muirfield, a spinster of inspirational get-up-and-go, achieved the status of living legend. The story goes that Moira, for many years the doyen of the Grange's popular handicraft club, started knitting a Fair Isle jumper during *Homes Under the Hammer* and was casting off before they got to the Mystery House in *Escape to the Country*. "Formidable" is perhaps the adjective we're looking for here.

Given that Somerville Grange is without a doubt the perfect place to pass one's final years, even in this earthly paradise death will inevitably come calling at some point. But the Grangers are a stoic bunch, respectfully bidding farewell to old friends, while eagerly anticipating the exciting prospect of new arrivals to take their place.

Only rarely does the community dwell on any one passing, but Davy Park's death proved to be the exception to that rule, the circumstances of his demise gleefully remembered even now, years after the event

Davy, a widower well into his eighties, had for over a decade passed his days in placid contentment. All went well until Sandra Parkinson arrived at the Grange. There were some, chiefly among the more prissy residents, who surmised Sandra had what they darkly referred to as a "back story". Fact was, Sandra was a bit of a stunner. Even in her late sixties she had all the allure of a woman half her age. Heads turned when she passed, among them Davy Park's.

It turned out to be a case of fatal attraction. Having wooed and won the fair maiden, or, in the opinion of some, been seduced by her sluttish charms, Davy then took her to bed. Sadly, the unaccustomed excitement proved too much for his octogenarian heart which gave out at the moment of climax. Ever since, Davy Park has been remembered as the man who came and went at the same time.

Naturally, you'll find no mention of death in the Somerville Grange brochure. As upbeat in its promises as in practice, the emphasis is on living the good life. We all know we can't take it with us, so where better to cash in your chips than in such amenable surroundings with so many interesting neighbours?

It's my intention to become a regular visitor to Somerville Grange and report on the many and varied activities of the indomitable resident characters. You are cordially invited to join me. I hope you will.

TWO
ALICE

After the death of her husband, Alice Nolan decided to make a new start. She'd been married to Jim for coming on fifty years, and though it seemed Jim had spent more time at the golf club, they'd lived in the same house in the same area for most of that time. The truly tragic aspect of her husband's demise was that it had come soon after the death of her great confidante and life-long friend, Mary. Doubly bereft, and with her two girls happily living their own independent lives, Alice bravely came to the conclusion that it wasn't too late to try something new.

So when Myra, Alice's elder daughter, came across an advertisement extolling the virtues of the Somerville Grange Retirement Complex, and tentatively suggested her mother might investigate the possibilities, she was amazed and delighted by Alice's positive reaction.

It took Alice only one visit to make up her mind. Enchanted by the peaceful setting in the softly wooded valley with the charming flats and chalets clustered round the placid lake, Alice knew, after years of teasing about her name, she had at long last found her wonderland.

Only two days after moving into her new home, Alice was even more certain she'd made the right move. She'd been warmly welcomed on her arrival by cheery representatives from various groups and organisations, eagerly informing her about the wide range of activities on offer at Somerville Grange.

Always eager for new blood, the Grangers, as they liked to think of themselves, had every reason to be pleased with the new arrival. Alice, although into her seventies, was petite and attractive, with a tidy cap of blonde hair. Although her figure had lost the voluptuous perfection of her younger days, in the opinion of at least one old fellow, she was still "well upholstered". Not perhaps quite the words he used, but you get the idea.

Towards the end of the first week in her new home, in need of a few essential bits and bobs, Alice took advantage of the bus service which ran three days a week, to visit the local town. The bus left early in the morning and returned from the town at three in the afternoon.

By one o-clock, Alice had completed her shopping and, with a couple of hours to spare, decided to treat herself to a mid-day bite in the restaurant of a large department store. Unfortunately, she wasn't the only one with that in mind. There must have been at least a dozen other shoppers with the same idea, all of them lined up at the entrance to the tearoom. However, even as Alice contemplated trying elsewhere, a chubby, humourless waitress, obviously charged with the task of keeping the queue moving, impatiently chivvied the folks at the front to recently vacated tables. Alice, who used to annoy her husband with her habit of labelling perfect strangers with nicknames, immediately christened this bossy individual "The Commandant".

Bossy The Commandant may have been, but no one could have complained she wasn't efficient and it wasn't long before Alice found herself at the head of the queue.

'Table for two,' barked The Commandant, bearing down on

Alice. Until then, Alice hadn't been aware of the elderly gentleman behind her. Obviously the waitress had assumed they were together. 'Table for two!' she snapped, louder this time, in the fond belief she was addressing yet another pair of doolally oldies.

And that was the magic moment. With only the faintest shrug and the raising of one eyebrow, the old chap communicated volumes; acknowledging the farcical situation, implying 'fine by me if you don't mind' and the imperative warning of 'better not rub *her* the wrong way.'

'Well, come on then!' thundered The Commandant. 'What are you waiting for?'

So a table for two it was. By the time their order was served, Alice and David – who had introduced himself as David Young but was usually referred to as young David – were chatting away as though they'd known one another all their lives. Only a few years older than Alice, David had a friendly, lived-in face. What hair he had remaining suggested he might once have been a redhead and, as Alice had instantly realised, he had a droll and impish sense of humour.

When eventually The Commandant brusquely tendered the bill, there were no arguments as to who might pay. Gallantly, David insisted and Alice gracefully agreed, but with the proviso that next time the treat would be on her.

After that, the magical day got even better. When Alice regretfully announced she had to catch the bus back to Somerville Grange at three-o-clock, the seemingly unflappable David was, for a moment, lost for words. At various points during their cosy confab in the restaurant they'd found so much in common that the expression "it's a small world" had cropped up more than once, but now they realised just how small the world really was.

There was no need for Alice to rush off for the bus, David assured her, for the simple reason that he was also a resident at

Somerville Grange, and they could travel back together in his car. Alice was speechless. Until then, Alice had thought of her move to Somerville Grange as being some sort of epilogue, but suddenly it had turned out to be the beginning of a brand-new chapter.

Not long after that, the happy couple were dining together once more, this time in the more intimate setting of Alice's cosy new home. When inevitably the moment came to consummate their friendship, Alice stood playfully at the open bedroom door. 'Come on then!' she commanded. 'What are you waiting for?'

THREE

THE SOMERVILLE PLAYERS

'...And that was his downfall!' The words were declaimed by a be-whiskered gentleman, wearing a deer-stalker hat and holding in his hand an enormous magnifying glass. Almost immediately the curtain fell. Unfortunately, it would have been better if the curtain had simply closed, as it should have done. Luckily, this was only a rehearsal for Gavin Madison's latest extravaganza, to be performed by the am-dram enthusiasts, a motley mix known collectively as the Somerville Players, in the luxurious retirement complex. Accidents like this were pretty much par for the course in any theatrical enterprise overseen by the thespian guru of Somerville Grange. Looking on the bright side, it wasn't all bad news, at least no one was injured... this time.

Twice a year, the Players entertained their fellow Grangers with productions masterminded by Gavin Madison; that is to say, produced, directed and, ever since the acrimonious dispute with the Performing Rights Society, even written by the great man himself. Gavin would be the first to admit he was one of the old-school types; kitchen sink dramas and angry young men might have appealed to some, but Gavin remained faithful to the cosy domestic comedies he'd first come across as a member of the local Village Dramatic Society. The man was a walking anachronism; his wardrobe looked as if it had been bought by his mother sometime in the Fifties and never since updated. There was, though, the off-chance that the heavy horn-rimmed glasses he favoured might one day come back into fashion.

The plots of Gavin's alleged comedies hinged on barely credible misunderstandings, featuring domineering matriarchs, posh twits and silly-ass vicars with unreliable braces. A dismally outdated format, but surprisingly popular with the Grangers.

Sadly, it wasn't Gavin's not so witty one-liners or the woefully unfunny plots which were the source of their mirth; there was much more entertainment to be had from the ridiculous spectacle of juvenile leads being played by an arthritic septuagenarians, the wobbly scenery, missed cues and wayward props, and, topping it all, the unintentional hilarity of the occasional musical accompaniment provided by Elsie Blair, who had obviously been given piano lessons by the late Les Dawson.

On the other hand, The Somerville Players were blessed with the presence of a glamorous leading lady, Gloria Goodwood, a blonde bombshell, languid and curvaceous, her sex appeal undiminished by advancing years. Gloria, whose real name, Martha Carson, no one ever mentioned, never missed a chance to let you know she'd featured in early episodes of *The Bill* and *Casualty*, artfully omitting the fact that they were non-speaking roles.

There was of course a downside to having such an experienced actress in the cast, which was that her excellence, in relative terms, only highlighted the abysmal standard of the others. Not that Gloria allowed their inadequacies to affect the quality of her leading roles; let the others stumble and mumble, she had her reputation to consider! Like a beacon in the darkness, performance after performance Gloria Goodwood rose to the challenge, her acting, in her opinion at least, deserving the awards regularly given to less worthy, but better-known, stars.

The Grangers loved her and one performance in particular will never be forgotten, Gloria was starring in the titular role of Gavin Madison's epic historical romance, *His First Love,* a period drama in which the dashing Lord Featherstone, a serial seducer of beautiful women, on a weekend visit to Baron Buckland's opulent country house, comes across the long-lost love of his life, Clarissa Wodehouse.

Surprisingly for a Somerville Players production, despite the ridiculous plot, the play had been well received, so it was doubly unfortunate that on the last night the actor playing the dashing Lord was taken ill and the only person who could be persuaded to take his place was the diminutive Charlie Cook. Five foot two, without a hair on his head, a timid wee man with a stage presence rivalled only by the standard lamp in the corner of the set, Charlie was as unlike a serial seducer as could be imagined.

At the start of the second act, the ludicrously ill-matched lovers, seeking a private place for a bit of hanky-panky, collude to meet secretly in the Baron's library only to discover the Baron already there. In a passage laden with clumsy double-entendres, the romantic tension is racked up until, realising he's obstructing the course of true love, the Baron does the decent thing and decides to make himself scarce. Unfortunately, on this occasion his attempt to exit stage left was undone when he was unable to open the door. Tugging with increasing force, he eventually pulled the door down, rendering himself unconscious and, in a domino effect, causing the collapse of two more flats.

Within seconds, three stagehands and even Gavin Madison himself leaped onto the stage in a desperate attempt to restore the stricken set. Disaster, it seemed, had struck again. But all was not yet lost. Cometh the hour, cometh the old trooper; no one knew better than she that the show must go on.

Heedless of the comatose Baron and the sweating

stagehands, Gloria Goodwood strode across the stage. Bristling with carnal intent, she clasped the bewildered Charlie Cook to her magnificent bosom and uttered the immortal line: 'At last, we are alone!'

Of course it's unlikely that even the Somerville Players could ever reach such heights again, but their loyal followers lived in hope. You can be sure that when the curtain – restored to its proper place – opens on the first night of Gavin Madison's exciting whodunit, *Mid-Winter Murders,* featuring his detective creation, Shylock Mansions, it will be standing room only in the former ballroom at Somerville Grange.

FOUR

THE WILD WEST

It was a wet morning at Somerville Grange, so the usual straggle of old codgers were stranded in what they rather grandly referred to as the clubhouse. There would have been a time, before they retired to the cosseted comfort of the palatial retirement home, when they might well have passed a wet morning looking out onto a rain sodden fairway, waiting for the clouds to clear, in the stuffy confines of a golf-club.

On this dismal morning, however, the old guys were quite happy to pass the morning in what, in the Grange's former glory days, had been a frivolous folly, a miniature castle, replete with crenulated façade. This commodious outhouse had, in summers long past, hosted fanciful garden parties, but was now relegated to the role of superior – remember we're at Somerville Grange, so *vastly* superior – man shed.

The interior was luxuriously fitted out with comfy armchairs and recliners and no expense had been spared on the carpets. A giant television screen took up most of one wall and of course the folly was centrally heated. You could have travelled many a mile to find a more agreeable spot in which to pass a wet morning.

Seated in their favourite armchairs overlooking the immaculate lawn were Jim Curtis and Tommy Dale, two long-time residents of the Grange, both now well into their seventies, and as easy in one another's company as an old married couple. Tommy was checking out the morning news on his tablet, a habit Jim thought of as rather an affectation, his preference being for a real newspaper.

'Saw a good film on the telly last night,' ventured Jim, hoping Tommy might put the tablet aside. 'An old John Wayne picture. *The Searchers.*'

His gamble paid off. 'That's going back a bit, you don't see a lot of Westerns nowadays.'

'That's a fact. Used to be, every time you went to the pictures they'd be showing Cowboys and Indians. Remember all the big stars? Hopalong Cassidy, Buffalo Bill and Roy Rogers. I liked Roy Rogers and good old Trigger.'

Fully engaged now, Tommy laid aside his tablet. 'What about Tex Ritter? The girls used to get angry when we called him Rex Titter.' Both laughed, remembering innocent times.

'My favourite was Kit Carson. He was in *Custer's Last Stand,* one of the serials at the *ABC Minors.*'

'That takes me back,' sighed Tommy. 'I used to go every Saturday morning. Great days.'

'I could never stand tapioca.'

Somewhat bemused, Tommy and Jim looked to their left. Dave Simpson had been sitting there when they'd arrived; they'd exchanged civil greetings but no more. Dave was a relative newcomer and had given the impression of being a bit of a loner, or even, to give him the benefit of the doubt, a bit on the shy side. On previous occasions when Tommy and Jim had attempted to bring him into their conversations, his responses had been monosyllabic or even obscure, giving the impression that, as Jim's mother might have said, *he wasn't the full shilling.*

'Who said anything about tapioca?' asked Jim, sharing a puzzled look with Tommy.

'You were talking about custard,' said Dave, obviously surprised they hadn't made the connection.

'We were talking about General Custer,' explained Tam.

'General George Custer, the guy who was massacred at the battle of the Little Big Horn,' added Jim, who was stickler for historical accuracy. He could have saved his breath, Dave was a man with a one-track mind.

'I don't mind custard, but I could never get a taste for tapioca, it was like eating frog spawn.'

Tommy and Jim, not wishing to seem impolite, nodded their vague agreement and returned to their original discussion.

'As I was saying, about the Saturday Morning Picture Show, remember how we used to cheer on the Goodies, as though it was a football match?'

'That's right. And we used to boo at the sloppy bits.'

'I don't mind rice, but you've got to be careful, you can easily go wrong with rice.' Dave nodded sagely, ploughing his own particular furrow.

Jim and Tommy exchanged exasperated glances.

'How do I get the impression you're going to tell us why we have to be careful with rice?' Tommy voiced what was in Jim's mind.

Getting into his stride, Dave leaned forward, his manner now confidential and expansive.

'You didn't know my wife, Jean.'

'No, we never met her,' Jim confirmed, his polite reply drowning out a sarcastic remark from Tommy, expressing pity for the poor woman.

'She was a great one for cooking fancy dishes, was Jean. She liked trying out erotic recipes.'

'Liked a bit of the hot stuff, did she?' asked Tommy innocently. Jim tried to not laugh.

'Her speciality was Pot Noodle and chips.'

'Sounds delightful,' said Jim, still trying to keep a straight face.

'She had a go at Indian cooking one time. Opened a tin of Kama Sutra curry.'

'Now *that* would be erotic,' Tommy solemnly agreed.

Dave was on a roll now. 'Trouble was, you know how you should have rice with curry? Well, Jean used rice pudding by mistake. And that's why you should always be careful with rice.'

'Well, thanks for sharing that with us, Dave,' said Jim, 'we'll keep that in mind.'

Having had his say, Dave stretched out in his chair and returned to his own reverie.

There was a pause while the other two exchanged surreptitious glances, then Tommy tentatively returned to the original subject. 'As I was about to say, there was a spell, you'll remember, when we had a lot of musical Westerns; *Calamity Jane, Seven Brides for Seven Brothers* and that sort of thing.'

'I remember it well. Some of them were quite good, if you liked Howard Keel, that is. Seems to me he was in every single one.'

'He wasn't in *Paint Your Wagon*. But that wasn't up to much.'

'I quite liked it.' Surprising them both, Dave spoke again.

'You liked *Paint Your Wagon*?'

'No. I liked curry and rice pudding. We used to have it quite often.'

It was obvious there would be no more talk about western films after that and, somewhat fortuitously, it was time return to their homes to see what their wives might have prepared for lunch. 'Let's go,' said Jim. 'If our luck's in, we might get something erotic.'

FIVE

BOBBY

The walled garden at Somerville Grange, situated behind the original manor house, might be thought of as one of its minor attractions. Modest by the standards of some fanciful rivals, this shaded nook nevertheless delivers on all the essentials required of a restful and secluded retreat. Enclosed by a weather-beaten wall of ancient undressed brick, the gardens are set around clusters of slim trees, shrubs and fondly tended flower beds; with wooden benches placed at regular intervals along the well-trodden gravel paths.

Although it was early yet to be sitting out – it would be a couple of weeks before the clocks went forward – Bobby Cowan, zipped into a substantial fleecy jacket, settled in his favourite spot. The pale early spring sun, playing peek-a-boo with a succession of puffy white clouds, gladdened his heart with the promise of brighter, warmer days to come.

As ever when seated in this perfect spot, Bobby marvelled at the fortunate eventualities which had brought him to this happy pass, allowing him to idle his days in what his younger self would have described as 'the lap of luxury.' He remembered the house where he'd grown up, freezing on winter mornings before the miracle of central heating, at a time of ration books and power cuts. He thought of other, less fortunate children, born as he was when the world was at war, their young lives snuffed out by falling bombs and insurrection. How lucky he'd been to be born in the right place at the right time.

So many things had changed in his lifetime. His was the last generation to have grown up without television; even now he still thought it a marvel to have coloured moving pictures in his own home. Careworn housewives queuing anxiously for a sausage or two, could never in their wildest dreams have imagined the laden shelves in today's supermarkets, their clothes dowdy and threadbare, condemned to a routine of make do and mend.

Looking back, he smiled to himself as he recalled the Prime Minister who'd been mocked for saying, 'You've never had it so good.' He would have been more accurate if he'd gone on to say, 'You ain't seen nothing yet.' The Britain of today bore little resemblance to the country he'd known in his youth. As he never tired of saying, his was the luckiest generation ever born.

He wondered then, as he often did, if the youngsters of today realise just how fortunate they are. The other day, on a trip to a shopping mall, he'd been in full-blown grumpy-old-man mode. Tuts tripped off his tongue at the spectacle of conceited youths in ragged, tattered denims. They would never have been allowed to leave the house like that in his young day. He'd been saddened, too, by pretty young girls mouthing casual obscenities. What sort of homes did they come from? There was a time when you'd never have heard a girl swear in public, and even the proverbial trooper would have drawn a line at cursing in the presence of a woman. Something to do with woman's lib, he supposed.

In the mall that day, observing the endless procession of affluent shoppers, careless of their good fortune, the former child of austerity was shocked by the sight of well-shod women shelling out enormous sums for yet another pair of shoes. Smiling ruefully to himself, he had the grace to realise just what an old grouch he was. He smiled, too, when the thought occurred that there was a time when if you wanted to see a tattooed lady, you had to pay to get into a freak show. Did they really believe all that inking made them more attractive? He couldn't help thinking that there would come a day when they'd regret their impetuosity,

For a moment, the sun was eclipsed by a wispy cloud and a puff of wind scattered a cluster of last year's fallen leaves, sending them scurrying along the path, revelling in their posthumous freedom. Other Grangers strolled past, some stopping for a word or two, but soon he was alone again with his thoughts.

Memories, mere sensations, a litany of random moments startling in their clarity, tumbled through his mind. The smell of newly laid carpets in his early married days, chaotic bath times with their daughters on cosy winter nights, family shopping trips to Tesco in the rusting red Allegro.

Feeling drowsy now, his mind wandered, awash with cinematic flashes of long forgotten incidents, dredged from the well of his subconscious. Flushed with contentment, he nodded off, drifting into sleep, never to wake again.

SIX

THE THREE MISS MARPLES

They thought of themselves as the Three Miss Marples, although only one of them was, to use that outdated expression, a spinster, and that was Miss Agnes Morrison. The other two, Mary Powell and the serendipitously named Jane Douglas, were both widows, neither of them particularly merry, but at the same time seemingly content with their single state.

It was their shared enthusiasm for the mysteries of Agatha Christie that had brought the three of them together and, in particular, the stories featuring Miss Marple; so much so that they had formed an exclusive society with the intention of modelling their lives on that of their heroine.

In that respect, they could not have selected a better location than Somerville Grange to replicate the staid backwater that was St Mary Mead in the inter-war years. Here at the Grange, time stood still, all wheeled traffic was prohibited, cars were parked on the perimeter and the houses and cottages were designed to give the impression of a sleepy English village, complete with roses round the doors and ivy on the walls.

Life would have been perfect for our Three Miss Marples, but for one inconvenient fact. Whereas in St Mary Mead residents and visitors tended to fall like flies, apart from the odd fatal heart attack, sudden death was a rarity in this tranquil retreat. Jane Douglas would later claim the credit for solving that particular problem, although Mary Powell, who maintained a tight-lipped silence whenever that fact was mentioned, seemingly thought otherwise.

Whoever came up with the idea, it was eagerly accepted by the others. What Jane, or perhaps Mary, proposed was that there was murder aplenty on the telly, so why not hone their detective skills in solving those ready-made murder mysteries? Since most series ran to six episodes, the trio would meet regularly to discuss the story so far and speculate on who might be guilty of the latest dastardly deed. Over time, they boasted a respectable degree of success, congratulating themselves on their ability to match their heroine's achievements, conveniently ignoring the fact that as a rule, three heads are better than one.

In yet another way, the impression of living the rosy-hued lifestyle enjoyed by the residents of St Mary Mead was enhanced by their "own little treasure" in the person of Tanya Miller, the Romanian wife of Jack Miller, the head maintenance man at the Grange. Just as Jane Marple and her contemporaries had girls from the village "to do" for them, Tanya, albeit unwittingly, performed that function, carrying out household chores two days a week for each of the Miss Marples in turn.

In her early thirties, Tanya was often bemused by the behaviour of the three mad ladies, as she thought of them. She was puzzled by their obsessions; constant references to red herrings and trips up garden paths. Not that she bothered too much about their eccentricities; for the most part, she was happy just to get on with her work. Only once did Tanya have any cause for concern.

On that particular occasion, Mary Powell was absent from the normal afternoon gathering and in reply to Tanya's polite enquiry, Jane Douglas somewhat vaguely suggested, 'She's... err... gone up to town.'

'Gone to see a man about a dog!' added Agnes, tapping the side of her nose and giving Tanya a confidential nod.

Tanya was horrified. For days after, she fretted, dreading the arrival of the pet. At the same time the thought occurred to her that, since Mary Powell was suffering from a gynaecological problem at the time, it seemed a particularly inopportune moment to acquire a dog.

However, weeks passed and in time Mary's health improved and there was no more talk about a dog, which was just as well as Tanya had a pathological fear of animals.

'What's happened to your Hephalant?' asked Agnes.

The three were convened for their regular afternoon consultation, tucking into cream teas. Agnes pointed to Mary's fireplace where the ornamental ivory elephant, no bigger than a hand, habitually took pride of place.

Mary, her features enhanced by a cream moustache, was speechless for a second.

'It was there last week,' volunteered Jane.

'It's not there now,' gasped Mary, inelegantly transferring the cream from her face to the back of her hand.

'Well, that's a funny thing,' said Jane.

'There's nothing funny about it at all,' exclaimed Mary, 'that dear Hephalant – that Indian elephant is worth a pretty penny.'

'Yes, my dear, of course, I meant no offence. The strange thing is that only this morning, I noticed my Georgian carriage clock was missing.'

Not to be outdone, Agnes added her pennyworth. 'You're not going to believe this, but you know my crystal scent bottle, the one my mother left me? That's missing, too.'

'I say! You don't think we've been burgled?' gasped Jane. 'Who could have done such a thing?'

After a moment, Mary gave voice to what they'd all been thinking. 'There's only one person who has access to all our homes, but I'm sure it can't be Tanya. Not our little treasure?'

'Who else might it be?' said Agnes. 'Look at it this way, she has a free run of our houses. For a girl like that, think of the temptation. She must surely realise how much those treasures are worth.'

'Oh, but not our Tanya! I can't believe she'd do a thing like that,' said Jane. 'It's just too awful. Think of the consequences. If we report the thefts and our suspicions, Tanya and her husband will not only be dismissed, they'll lose the house that goes with his job, too.'

Agnes took a moment to refresh the teacups, then proposed they give the matter more thought. 'Don't let's jump to any hasty conclusions. Let's give ourselves time to consider the situation before we do anything we might regret.'

At last it seemed that the Miss Marples had a genuine mystery to solve, but not in a manner they would have wanted. It was then agreed that they should wait until next they met to decide on a course of action.

The next meeting convened at Jane's house which, considering the gravity of the situation, was particularly unfortunate. Jane, to put it mildly, was not best pleased that morning. She'd recently been duped into paying rather a lot for a painting she though was an original, which, when she got it home, turned out to be only a print. She was therefore disinclined towards leniency.

'It's my opinion the girl's guilty, and we should waste no more time. I vote we take our complaint to the Main Office.'

'And Mary, do you agree with Jane?' asked Agnes.

'Regretfully, I see no other option than to report the matter.'

Conscious of the seriousness of the situation, Mary and Jane were surprised to see a smile on Agnes's face, a smile that rapidly grew into what Miss Marple herself would probably have described as a chortle.

Mary was aghast. 'Really, Agnes my dear, I'm surprised at you, this is no laughing matter.'

'You really are a pair of silly-billies,' laughed Agnes. 'You should surely know by now that the most obvious suspect is never the guilty party.'

'Whatever do you mean?'

'Who else might it have been?'

'I'll give you a clue.' So saying, Agnes reached into her shopping bag and withdrew the Indian elephant and the carriage clock.

'But didn't you lose something, too?' asked Mary, still looking puzzled.

'It's the oldest trick in the book. The guilty party pretends to be a victim, too.' Smug as a two- tailed cat, Agnes revelled in their dismay.

'That really was despicable,' griped Jane, still smarting from the business about the painting, and even more annoyed by her friend's duplicity. 'To think we might have caused so much distress for that poor girl.'

'But we didn't, did we? And look on the bright side, you've got your treasures back, and we've still got Tanya, our own little treasure.'

Later that night, blissfully unaware of her starring role in *The Mystery of Somerville Grange*, Tanya tossed and turned in her bed, unable to sleep. The following day she was due at Jane Douglas's house. Miss Douglas had been in a foul mood lately, but that wasn't the cause of Tanya's concern, she was used to coping with the prissy ways of "her ladies". The cause of Tanya's restlessness was an exchange she'd overheard between Mrs

Powel and Mrs Morrison and something they'd said about Miss Douglas.

'Where?' wondered the sleepless Tanya. 'Where would it be kept? Would she be expected to clean up after it? And what about the smell?' No matter how hard she tried, the same questions ran through her mind, rendering sleep impossible.

It was past three in the morning before she finally got to sleep, but only after her husband, Jack, disturbed by her restlessness, explained the meaning of the expression, "buying a pig in a poke".

SEVEN

INFATUATION

J im Curtis closed the door behind him and, tidy chap that he was, hung his jacket carefully in the wardrobe, before stretching out in his recliner. The luxurious leather-bound chair was perfectly positioned in the living room of his small but elegant flat, bordering the tree-fringed lake at Somerville Grange. He needed only to swivel left or right to take advantage of the glorious, ever-changing outlook or to line up with the outrageously large television screen, taking up a disproportionate amount of space in one corner. Jim's happiest hours were spent in what one of his grandchildren called "Papa's Throne".

Yet this afternoon Jim was troubled by a feeling of disquiet, wishing now that he'd spoken up. Instead, his silence had tacitly aligned him with the teasing Dave Simpson had been getting from the half dozen or so residents gathered in the opulent men's club room, in the old folly.

In an attempt to justify his inaction, he tied to persuade himself Dave had only himself to blame for the situation. Not the smartest cookie on the block, Dave, setting himself up for ridicule, had let his infatuation with Gloria Goodwood become common knowledge.

Gloria Goodwood was the impossibly glamorous star of the Somerville Players, the community's amateur dramatic society. The sad fact of the matter was that, given the best will in the world, no one could ever imagine a sex bomb like Gloria giving a somewhat dim and wimpish chap like Dave a second glance. Jim, uncomfortable with the teasing which threatened to get out of hand, like Sunday newspaper reporters of old, had made an excuse and left.

Settled now in the recliner, Jim allowed himself a secret smile, remembering a time when he, too, had been infatuated. It was a long time ago, so long ago he'd all but forgotten how besotted he'd been with Linda Murray. Lying back, he put his feet up, looking out across the lake and staring back down the years. In his mind, he was transported to that wonderful long-ago summer.

It's a popular misconception that the summers of our youth were sun-drenched idylls, an unbroken succession of languorous days, but the summer of 1955, when Jim was fourteen years old, was exactly like that.

Throughout July and August that year, under cloudless skies, Jim and his friends slouched daily by the swings in the park. Boys with downy cheeks and rough men's voices, trading juvenile insults and pooling their insubstantial knowledge of the procreational process.

Then, as fresh and exuberant as the bursting summer blooms, the girls appeared. Alien creatures; a giggling gaggle of post-pubescent femininity, with an awesome power Jim couldn't quite define. And among the girls was Linda Murray.

Outshining even the sun that glorious summer, Linda was a dark-haired, dark-eyed beauty, her radiant smile by turn sweet or wanton. Her voice was a delight, given more allure by just the hint of a lisp. Graceful by nature and lithe as a leopard on the tennis court, Linda arrived in a swirl of seersucker skirts and Jim was instantly besotted.

Some of his friends fancied Norma, a well-developed lass with bouncing breasts, while others lusted after Helen, a tarty little minx, rumoured to have few inhibitions. But Jim had eyes only for the lovely Linda; he was in love for the very first time.

Sighing at the memory, Jim rose from his chair, poured himself a neat whisky, then settled down again to his reverie.

There were other new experiences that summer. Under cover of limp-leafed trees, by the side of the all-but-dried-up river, Jim and his friends puffed and choked on pilfered Capstans and Players, the first cigarettes they'd ever smoked. On more affluent days, he remembered occasionally splashing out on a flimsy paper pack of five skinny Woodbines.

Shaking his head now at the absurdity of his behaviour, he recalled the times he'd spent in front of the mirror, rehearsing his Robert Mitchum look, nonchalantly dangling a pencil from the corner of his mouth. In practice though, the stinging taste of the tobacco was vile and the smarting smoke brought tears to his eyes.

When Linda, whose ambition was to become a nurse, declared her contempt for this unhealthy habit, he had stopped smoking immediately. So great was his infatuation at the time that, if Linda had disapproved of eating, he would have gladly starved to death. On a more practical level, he couldn't really afford to squander so much of his meagre pocket money on cigarettes.

He had been paid then for his work with the local butcher. In term time he made five shillings on Saturday mornings, but during the holidays he augmented that sum by putting in an hour each day.

It was no hardship on these fine sunny mornings to be out and about on the solid butcher's bike with the stout basket slotted in front of the handlebars. Even now, he remembered the pleasure, at the end of the week, of getting his hands on that precious ten-bob note.

A common belief among Jim's friends at that time was that, sooner or later, every delivery boy would eventually be confronted by an older, experienced woman. This seductively dressed vamp would lure innocent young lads to her boudoir, there to have her evil way with them. Looking back now, he was amused that his fourteen-year old self had vowed, if confronted by such a situation, to virtuously decline the invitation, priggishly letting it be known his heart belonged to another.

Other memories poured in. The accumulated succession of scorching, sunlit days produced suffocating, airless nights. As though it were yesterday, he recalled his sweltering, airless bedroom, stinking with the stench of sweaty adolescence. Alone there, he would review the events of the day, cherishing Linda's every word and move, never for a moment doubting the next day would be just as perfect as the last, and Linda would be there.

And so the wonderful, careless days had passed and even now when he heard the trumpet intro to *Cherry Pink and Apple Blossom White*, a popular song of the time, it brought to mind that glorious summer and Linda, the very first love of his life.

Then inevitably, that long-ago September dawned, with milky-misted mornings. School and responsibility beckoned. Tragically, Linda attended a different school and it would be a whole week until he would next see her, a lifetime away.

All these years later, he experienced again the utter desolation he'd felt that afternoon, the excruciating pang of loss and regret. The seemingly endless blazing days had slipped away, the long hot summer was over, and in all that time Linda Murray never once looked his way.

EIGHT

THE KNOW-ALLS

Perhaps the most popular communal activity among the residents at Somerville Grange was the weekly quiz night. Every Thursday, teams of five would take on the resident panel of quizzers led by Noel Davidson, a bookish chap with a penchant for gaudy bowties. From week to week, there might be some changes in the regular all-male line-up, but the ever-present star turn was "Professor" Alexander Sinclair, an astonishingly well-informed gentleman, reputed to have a photographic memory. To his credit, The Professor, a ginger nut with bushy red beard and wild hair to match, bore his erudition lightly, earning respect and approval in equal measure.

As a matter of expediency, to avoid any confusion with a similar competition shown nightly on television, and given the fact the leader was called Noel, the team went under the name of The Know-alls.

The Thursday night quizzes were a great success, drawing large audiences, some to support friends in the challenging teams, others simply come to marvel at the depth of The Professor's knowledge. And then there was the indisputable bonus that the quizmaster was the accident-prone Gavin Madison.

Gavin Madison, with his old tweed jackets and horn-rimmed glasses, was well known to the Grangers through his work with the drama group, The Somerville Players. As writer, producer and director, he worked mostly behind the scenes with the Players, but at the weekly quizzes he was up front and centre stage. Not ideally the place to be if you habitually misplaced the cards with the questions. Nor was that his most embarrassing trait, as it soon became apparent that Gavin suffered from a mild form of dyslexia, resulting in some epic mispronunciations. On one gleefully remembered occasion, he brought the house down with his mangled version of the word for slow burning coal; anthracite. To say Gavin Madison was a poor man's Jeremy Vine would be an insult to poor men everywhere.

Jeremy Vine, in case you're wondering, is the question master of the television quiz show, *Eggheads*. (Oops! There, I've said it.)

Nevertheless, Noel Davidson's Know-alls were a competent bunch, and all went well until that redoubtable matron, Moira Muirfield, complained about the all-male line-up in the team and came up with the disruptive suggestion that it was time for change. *Miss* Muirfield, if you please – a gaunt crusader for the rights of women – insisted she should be given the chance to challenge the supremacy of the Know-alls with her all female team, called The Pinks. It wouldn't be the first time The Pinks had challenged the resident panel; like other teams composed of like-minded residents, they had competed against the Know-alls several times, and had even emerged victorious on one occasion.

The Pinks were indeed a formidable team, composed mainly from members of Moira's handicraft club which congregated in the television lounge, benefiting from the daily dose of trivia on afternoon telly. With a growing number of supporters, Moira eventually persuaded the Social Committee to arrange a Grand Challenge, a "best of three" competition between the Know-alls and the Pinks, the winner to be declared the resident team for the next six months.

To begin with, The Pinks drew their support mainly from the female Grangers, the men naturally backing Noel Davidson's team. That was before Moira Muirfield played her masterstroke, dumbfounding friend and foe alike, by displacing the timid wee woman whose name no one could remember, with the resident sex goddess of Somerville Grange, Gloria Goodwood. At a stroke, a number of men changed their allegiance and a likewise number of women, those who disapproved of Gloria's overt sensuality, did likewise.

To no one's surprise, The Know-alls won the first game; then, thanks in no small measure to Gloria Goodwood's brilliant head-to-head victory over the "Professor", the Pinks tied the series at one game all.

With all to play for, the Grange seethed with excitement. It was decreed that the decider would be an all-ticket affair, and such was the fervour among the supporters of the competing teams that it became an immediate sell-out. On the night, the doors were closed half an hour before proceedings were due to start, the atmosphere in the old hall as electric as the build-up to an FA Cup-tie.

As the game proceeded, the tension mounted. After the head-to-heads, the Pinks had lost three members, with only Moira Muirfield and Gloria Goodwood left facing the might of the Know-alls, including "Professor" Alexander Sinclair and Noel Davidson himself.

Gloria again excelled and after three questions the score was three-all. The noise and the excitement mounted, every point won by their favourites greeted in raucous fashion by the rowdy audience.

Having difficulty making himself heard at times, Gavin Madison upped the stakes dramatically. 'You no longer have the option of multiple choice,' he portentously announced. Then, turning to the Pinks, he read out their question. The Iron Maiden and the Blonde Bombshell immediately came up with the correct answer. Bedlam ensued and it was several minutes before order could be restored, allowing Gavin Madison to continue.

The contest stood on a knife-edge; all rested on the next question. Noisily clearing his throat ,Gavin proceeded. 'Corunna was a battle in which war?' Almost contemptuously, the "Professor" drawled his answer; 'The Peninsular War.'

'Incorrect!' yelped Gavin, then, reading from the card, he declaimed, 'The battle of Corunna was a battle of the Neapolitan War.'

'You mean the Napoleonic War, you nitwit and that included the Peninsular War!' shouted Noel Davidson, barely heard above the victorious cheers from the Pink following.

On the platform, the Pinks exchanged rather unladylike high fives and, for no discernable reason, a section of their supporters broke into a chorus of 'We're all going to Wembley', countered by opposition cries of 'Cheats! Cheats!' and 'We was robbed!'

Desperately attempting to restore order, Gavin Madison only succeeded in drawing the fire of both factions, who united in a hand-clapping, foot-stamping rendition of 'You don't know what you're doing!'

Eggheads was never like this.

As a result of the disgraceful scenes in the old ballroom, at its next meeting the Social Committee came up with three recommendations. (1) The Thursday night quizzes would be suspended for a period of two months. (2) The Know-alls would henceforth have to include at least two women in their team. The most telling change of all was (3); Gavin Madison would no longer retain the position of quizmaster, his place to be taken, with a potent mix of highbrow and low neckline, by none other than the glamorous Gloria Goodwood.

Eat your heart out, Jeremy Vine.

NINE

BRYAN AND MARGARET

'Your place or mine?' was never an option as far as Margaret Fellows was concerned. Even when it became obvious that she and Bryan Nugent would become lovers sooner rather than later, she still felt constrained by the moral code instilled in her, in her formative years. She felt guilty that so soon after her husband's death – less than a year, in fact – she should even be contemplating a new romance.

Bryan, who had been widowed for much longer, tried to reassure her, citing the many cases among the inhabitants of Somerville Grange, of older couples who had come together in much less time, for the obvious reason that, not to put too fine a point on it, at their late stage in life, there was a limit on how much time they might have left.

Still Margaret prevaricated. Her main objection concerned the fact that the entrance to her block of flats was overlooked by the bay windows of the television room, the daily haunt of the handicraft club. She had no wish to task Moira Muirfield and her gossip-happy cronies with the possibility of putting two and two together. For the same reason, she was loath to linger too long at Bryan's bungalow.

Which was a pity. Bryan and Margaret were a well-matched couple, she an elfin brunette with dark eyes to match, he a dapper little gent given to blazers and immaculately pressed flannels. Love had blossomed on Bonfire Night, an autumn romance, one might say, given the time of year and their respective ages.

Christmas had come and gone, and it was well into January when Margaret, feeling like a shameless hussy, came up with a possible solution.

'My cousin,' she began, not quite able to look Bryan in the eye, 'has a caravan, not far from here.' Bryan politely waited for her to continue. 'I spoke to her on the phone last night, and offered to give it an airing.'

'That was kind of you.' Bryan was trying to retain some dignity while sinking his gnashers into a generously filled bacon butty, and hadn't quite caught her drift.

'Don't you see? It would be the ideal place to meet, away from prying eyes. We could go there for... well, you know what.' There was an awkward pause, then, when the penny dropped, Bryan almost choked on his last bite.

He was in for an even greater shock when he arrived at the cousin's caravan, as the instant Bryan closed the door behind him, Margaret, who had travelled ahead in her own car, bundled him unceremoniously into the bedroom and on to the bed. Alas, her actions were prompted not by unbridled lust, but by the more basic human need for some warmth. The caravan, a delightful summertime residence, was quite the opposite in deep midwinter. A squall of driven sleet lashed against the picture windows and, lacking any kind of heating whatsoever, the marrow-chilling cold would have discomforted even the most intrepid Artic explorer.

But Bryan was an optimistic sort of chap. Sure, it wasn't quite as romantic as he'd imagined it might be, but here they were, in bed together at last!

It had been a long time since he'd found himself in intimate circumstances with a female other than his wife. That was in the decade before the swinging one when, it was alleged, sex had been invented.

In those far-off days there had been an accepted code of conduct. Having been given the green light by some enthusiastic snogging, etiquette decreed attention should then be given to his partner's breasts, before getting down to the nitty-gritty. Trouble was, access to Margaret's bosom was severely hindered by the number of minute buttons on the blouse she wore. Such buttons were fiddly things at the best of time, but given the fact that his more dexterous right hand was trapped uncomfortably under the object of his affection, it was proving well-nigh impossible.

Perhaps seeking to expedite matters, Margaret, putting to shame his own pathetic fumbling, deftly unzipped his fly. Only then did Bryan realise, with heart-stopping horror, that thanks to the Baltic chill in the caravan, she would find precious little within. He could have died of shame at that moment, and then, when Margaret laughed, he wished he had.

But there was no derision in her laughter, only wholesome mirth, inviting Bryan to share in the joke.

'For goodness' sake,' she giggled, 'whoever thought this was a good idea?' Then, in the wise words of worldly woman everywhere, she added: 'Let's just have a nice cup of tea.'

They didn't linger long over their cuppa, just long enough for Margaret to agree to shake off her inhibitions, and to hell with the gossipmongers. She then playfully assured him if he came calling the following Tuesday, he'd get a much warmer welcome.

Outside, Bryan gallantly cleared the slush from Margaret's windscreen and they embraced, taking their leave with a long and loving kiss, a kiss neither chaste nor carnal, and parted, not yet as lovers, but perhaps not for much longer.

To paraphrase Ira Gershwin; maybe Tuesday would be their good news day.

TEN

WILMA

It almost goes without saying that one has to be reasonably well-heeled to afford the upkeep of a property at Somerville Grange and many and varied are the roads to riches taken by the affluent residents. It would, however, be considered bad form to inquire too closely into any one person's circumstances, which is not to say speculation isn't rife.

A case in point was Wilma Greenhorn. Without being nasty about it, Wilma was thought of as being rather a rough diamond; always, though, with the proviso that she had a heart of gold. One person who could vouch for her kindliness was her friend and neighbour, Anna Fulton. That is, if Anna had still been able to speak. Anna had suffered a serious stroke and, as a consequence, had lost the use of her voice. She was grateful to Wilma for the concern she'd shown and for her daily visits.

Perhaps at first Wilma hadn't intended going into such detail about her life story, but once she started, she saw no reason to stop; after all, it wasn't as though her voiceless friend would go blabbing about it to anyone else.

'If my friends could see me now,' sighed Wilma one wet afternoon, on a visit to Anna's flat. 'The ones I had when I was young, I mean. They wouldn't believe it, me living the life of Riley in a posh place like this. I've had some hard times, I don't mind telling you. It wasn't always like this. I was what they called an unmarried mother. They call them single parents now. There's no shame to it nowadays, they give them child support and houses even. Nice work if you can get it, that's what I say. Back then, I had to look out for myself, for me and Lucy, that is. Me? I had to earn some money any way I could. Took up modelling, I did.'

Anna smiled encouragingly, wishing she could have joined in.

'You might not think it to look at me now, but back then I was sex on legs. Dare say I was lucky, the chap who took my pictures was one of these arty-farty types. "We're trying to create an impression of implied naughtiness," he'd say – that's saucy pics to you and me. 'Course I had to get my tits out, no harm in that, but I kept my knickers on. Say this for him, though, he wasn't the tactile type. Oh, I say, hark at me – "tactile", indeed! That's a word I heard on *Woman's Hour*, it means touchy-feely, but not gropey-like. I've met enough of them in my time, I can tell you.'

Anna nodded, showing she'd had her fair share of unwanted attention herself.

'It was through the modelling that I met Douglas,' continued Wilma. 'Lucky me. Douglas had a car showroom, selling expensive cars. They were launching a new model and me and another girl were the glamorous props, you know the kind of thing, tight sweaters and short skirts. Well, Douglas took a shine to me and asked me to marry him. Not quite as romantic as it sounds. You see Douglas was what these days they called a queer, a homosexual. Nowadays, it's all the rage to be gay, does you no harm at all, but back then you could end up in jail. Hard to believe that now. Point was, Douglas had to have a wife to take to all the business dos, mixing with the big money punters and all that.

'Best thing that ever happened to me. He doted on Lucy like she was his own and treated me like a queen, which is funny if you think about, being as he was the queen! If it wasn't for his money I wouldn't be here. 'Course you'll be wondering about my sex life, being as how he batted for the other side. Well, he was quite decent about that, too. I won't go into detail and maybe I shouldn't say this but, one way and another, I got my fair share.'

Wilma was quiet for a moment, perhaps thinking about some of the details. When she spoke again her tone was different, defensive almost.

'Maybe back then I felt some guilt about putting it about, but if you listen to the things they talk about on *Woman's Hour*, I reckon I must have been ahead of my time. Always going on about a woman's right to have an orgasm… I wish some of the blokes I knew had listened to that! There was a bit the other day about how age shouldn't be a barrier to sex, talking about sexually active oldies. It seems we're not supposed to just lie back and think of England, but at the same time they tell us not to go at it hammer and tongs. Remember that old fellow who popped his clogs on the job? Must have done their research at Somerville Grange.'

Anna looked at her quizzically.

'No need to look like that, I'm not past it yet. I've still got my needs. *Needs!* That's another word you hear a lot about on *Woman's Hour*. But don't you worry about me. I've got myself a boyfriend here, Dave Simpson. Some of the guys think he's a bit soft, but his heart's in the right place, along with a few other organs. If you take my meaning.

'Only thing I miss here is Lucy. She emigrated to Australia ages ago and of course I miss Douglas, too. Six years now since he died. I suppose in a manner of speaking you could say they're both down under.'

Although the trite comment didn't deserve it, there was a moment of reverential silence, broken by the clock by the fireplace chiming the hour.

'Goodness me, is that the time? I better be getting along, Dave's coming round tonight. I'm looking forward to it. We're having one of our tactile evenings.'

ELEVEN
FOUNDER'S DAY

One, two, one-two-three-four. The trumpet blasted the lead, the clarinet complimented the melodic line with a winsome counterpoint and the gruff trombone filled in the gaps. Behind them, the steady boom of the double bass, the sizzling cymbals and the persistent clunk of the banjo provided the rhythmic thrust and stomping beat of the trad band. Jazz on a summer's day.

The toe-tapping music brought happy smiles to the faces of the audience. Grangers and their visitors were gathered round the platform erected in front of the old manor house, bringing back memories of their teenage years when they'd jived to bands like this in smoky cellars and at tennis club hops.

It was the second Saturday in July, Founder's Day at The Grange, the ironic title given to the annual fête held on the anniversary of the opening of Simon Forsyth's ambitious venture. As ever, the great man was in attendance, accompanied by his wife and his two sons who now ran the business. The royal family, as it were.

Over the years, the annual celebration has mutated into a rather grand version of a village fête and mini sports day. Apart from the bandstand in front of the manor house, a large marquee stood on the lawns, part beer tent but mainly providing space for the Great Somerville Bake-off and entries in the various categories of flower arrangement. As you may have gathered, the Grangers are a pretty competitive bunch.

Outside, the sporting element consisted of the golf championship, in reality a putting contest on the fiendishly tricky, nine-holed crazy-golf course laid out beside the Walled Garden. Before that, there is the Lawn Bowls competitions; the most prestigious event because of its popularity as a sport played by both sexes.

Qualifying rounds are held in the weeks before the great day and even to reach the finals is deemed a notable achievement. This year, surprising herself as much as the perennial hopefuls, Alice Nolan, in her first year at the Grange and encouraged by her newfound lover and partner (in both senses of the word), David Young, had reached the final of the mixed doubles. In a closely contested match, much to the dismay of most of the spectators, they were narrowly beaten by the reigning champs, a humourless couple who had alienated too many by their grim determination on their way to the final.

On the putting green, Tommy Dale had an easier victory over another surprise finalist. Gavin Madison, more notable for his accident-prone thespian activities, had somehow beaten off all comers to feature in the play-off. His luck couldn't last, of course, and true to form he'd delighted the spectators with a typically disastrous performance when he'd achieved the seemingly impossible feat of racking up twelve shots on what was by far the shortest hole.

Elsewhere, the band played on and the sun shone on happy faces enjoying the once-a-year day. An assortment of the usual fairground booths lined the path to the lake, where enthusiastic anoraks snared unwary visitors with tedious details about their handcrafted model boats. The festive atmosphere enhanced the sense of belonging. Old friends were warmly greeted and new friendships forged. One rare exception was a resentful teenager, dragged against her will to spend the day among a bunch of geriatric has-beens. Making up for her sulky presence, there was the heart-warming sight of a tiny tot in a pushchair, trying to get to grips with the elusive sweetness on a wand of candy floss. Among the contented Grangers enjoying all the fun of the fair there was none happier than Wilma Greenhorn, whose daughter Lucy had arrived unexpectedly from down under with her hunky Aussie hubby.

Mixing with the crowd, the Three Miss Marples cajoled residents and visitors alike to try their luck in the raffle to win a cuddly toy dog. This they'd managed with moderate success, but it wasn't until the ultra-glamorous Gloria Goodwood decided to lend a hand that sales really took off. All the profits from the festive day would be donated to worthy causes – mostly, since the Grangers know just how fortunate they are, to charities for the homeless.

Meanwhile, in the marquee, Moira Muirfield judged the entries for the bake-off. Moira had been assigned to the task since it was the only way to stop her winning the competition every year. The winner on this occasion, an underwhelming challenge for the most original filling in a Victoria sponge, was the timid wee woman whose name no one could ever remember.

As the festivities drew to a close, the crowds congregated in front of the bandstand where, gracious as a countess, Emily Forsyth, the founder's wife, presented the cups and certificates to the day's winners. Then, as long-standing tradition decreed, her husband thanked one and all for their efforts in making the day a resounding success, and received in turn three rousing cheers.

There were some among the visitors who smiled indulgently at this rather quaint custom, but the Grangers are sticklers for tradition, their pride in the community bonded by the outdated practice, their sense of togetherness made all the stronger.

To round things off, the Jazz Band launched into a punchy rendition of the war-time ballad, *We'll Meet Again*. The Grangers joined in singing the emotional words, cherishing the memory of other places and other faces associated with the old favourite. Loving the sentimental moment and in defiance of old age and infirmity, they sang with single-minded assurance that they really would meet again some sunny day.

The perfect ending to yet another wonderful day at Somerville Grange.

TWELVE
A SPINSTER OF THE GREAT WAR

Massie Stevens sighed as she closed the curtains. The long, dark winter lay ahead. Already, the garden centres and the shopping malls were on full alert for Christmas, and Halloween was still a week away. These things seemed to come along earlier each year. It would be another three weeks until Remembrance Sunday and yet the television newsreaders were already wearing poppies. Armistice Sunday more like, Massie thought. She couldn't remember when they'd changed the name, but somehow the new title didn't seem right. Even in her younger days, long after the original eleventh hour of the eleventh day of the eleventh month, there were still family members and friends who had personal memories of that horrific war and who would never forget the relief and the sorrow of that long-awaited day.

She thought then, as she often did at this time of year, of her mother's maiden aunt, Aunt Jeanie. Not her favorite relative. Massie remembered her as a small, birdlike creature with the beady eyes of a combative bantam forever on the lookout for a fallen crumb. Massie had never been comfortable in her great-aunt's presence, but at that time she'd been too young to understand the ways of the world and how life wasn't always fair.

When she was young, Massie had only a hazy idea of Aunt Jeanie's circumstances. She was aware that, unlike the other women in the family who stayed at home looking after their children, her great-aunt had worked long shifts as a supervisor in a factory until shortly before she died. The one thing Massie remembered was that she'd been concerned when she'd heard Aunt Jeanie had moved into digs. In her childish mind, Massie had imagined the old woman living in a hole in the ground.

Older now and wiser, Massie realized there may well have been a reason for her great-aunt's sour demeanor. Like thousands of other women whose lives were blighted by the tragic repercussions of the war to end wars, Aunt Jeanie never married. Even in her own family she was a person to be pitied, a single woman left on the shelf, the butt of the comedian's cruel jibe: 'Born a spinster, lived a spinster, died a spinster, returned unopened.'

But how different her great-aunt's life might have been. What if she'd had "an understanding" with some young man? Perhaps one of those naïve Tommies, grinning from the old sepia prints, back bent under the weight of his old kit bag, marching as to war. A simple lad, his life barely lived, plucked by fate from the streets of the old mill town to be blown to smithereens on Flanders Fields.

How many nights, Massie wondered, after an arduous day in the factory, had her great-aunt fallen asleep, thinking of what might have been? Poor Aunt Jeanie.

Although among the Grangers there were few left who had seen active service, there were still some who'd done their square-bashing before National Service had been abolished. Enough to make a respectable parade to commemorate the fallen, whose sacrifice had made it possible for them to live in a land of the free. Massie wasn't a regular at the Sunday services held in the former ballroom, but she always made a point of attending on Armistice Sunday, or whatever they called it these days.

On these dark November mornings when we remember the millions senselessly slaughtered, she thought of the other victims, a generation of women cursed by coincidence, condemned to lead solitary, unfulfilled lives; women like her mother's maiden aunt, Aunt Jeanie, a spinster of the Great War.

May they rest in peace.

THIRTEEN
THE FASHIONISTA

The Scotts, Andrew and Betty, were long-time residents at Somerville Grange. They'd sold up home and business more than ten years previously, seduced by the prospect of a lengthy and comfortable retirement. Married now for nigh on fifty years, never for a moment had they regretted making the early move. Their children had long since flown the nest and they were free to enjoy the rewards of their lucrative enterprise; a kitchen gadget company, started in the proverbial garden shed, sold years later for a six figure sum. That said, they may well have been partners in business and marriage for almost half a century but that's not to say they were joined at the hip.

They were each determined to plough their own furrow; Betty never happier than in the company of her cohort of woman friends, chief among them Pam, an old chum from before her days at the Grange, now one of her neighbours. Together, Betty and Pam had recently joined the popular watercolour painting group, an activity they felt complimented the image of themselves as being a cut above the norm, in the same way as being members of the book club and making occasional appearances as bit part players in Gavin Madison's am-dram productions.

Betty and Pam also made regular visits to the nearby town, chiefly to the more up-market clothing stores. Not that either of them was in desperate need of something to wear, quite the opposite, but Betty in particular was a dedicated follower of fashion. It was a mystery to her husband why anyone with such a bulging wardrobe should ever need another outfit or yet another pair of shoes.

As for Andrew, he spent much of his time in the men's retreat in the Old Folly, enjoying the endless succession of sporting events shown on the supersized telly. In particular, he followed the fortunes of his hometown football club, just as he had in his pre-Grange days. The difference now being that he didn't have to travel all over the country as the games came to him.

For a couple who'd lived so long together, their resemblance to the Sprats, who'd had differing opinions about bacon, was a source of much amusement to their friends. Andrew could never, even after all these years, understand how his wife could be such a persistent pessimist. No glass was ever half full; if the sun shone in the morning, to Betty it was a sure sign it would be wet later. It was little wonder her husband often referred to her as 'She who must be dismayed.'

As far as Betty was concerned, her husband's greatest crime was his inability to understand the principle of colour coordination. More than that, he seemed to have no notion that fashions changed, being inclined to wear the same ill-matched outfits year after year. No matter how often she told him his idea of style was 'So last year', he would simply shrug a dismissive, 'So what?'

On one of her regular visits to her friend's house, Pam noticed she was looking particularly despondent, even for Betty.

'Penny for them,' invited Pam.

Betty confessed that she'd been thinking about the funeral of an old Scotsman and how it was the talk of The Grange that the old fellow had been laid out in his coffin wearing full Highland dress.

'Cheer me up, why don't you?'

'It made me wonder how on earth I would dress Andrew. He hasn't even got a good suit.'

Pam smiled. Only Betty Scott would find this a cause for concern, especially since there was an obvious answer: 'Why not just buy him one?'

'Of course!' Betty brightened, then, after a moment, looked worried again. 'But he mustn't find out.'

'Depend on me,' said Pam, who could never be serious for long. 'We'll keep it shrouded in secrecy.'

The matter of secrecy proved to be not quite as easy as it sounded; like mice and men, even the best laid schemes of women are apt to stray.

A few days later, soon after Andrew had left the house on a visit to the Folly, Pam sneaked in, eager to see what Betty had bought for her unsuspecting husband. It was indeed a fine garment, but even as the two friends admired the suit, disaster struck. Andrew returned unexpectedly to the house; he'd forgotten a book he'd promised one of his cronies.

There was a moment when time stood still, Betty frozen in horror, unable to conceal the new suit, Pam wide-eyed and open mouthed, and Andrew staring uncomprehendingly towards his wife.

He was first to recover. 'Is that a man's suit you've got there?' he asked. 'It's not for me, is it?'

'Well, yes... it's for...' Betty stumbled.

Pam came to her rescue. 'It's for a special occasion,' she said, then turned away, hand to her mouth, shoulders shaking with suppressed laughter.

Totally bemused, Andrew looked from one woman to the

other, shook his head and picked up the forgotten book. As he turned to leave, he realised that even though he hadn't asked Betty to buy him a new suit, it looked like rather nice and it would be impolite not to express some thanks.

As he closed the door behind him, Andrew heard an explosion of uncontrolled laughter, the two women howling like a pair of hysterical hyenas. He was totally bemused. He couldn't think of a special occasion coming up any time soon and all he'd said was that he expected he'd get a lot of wear out of the new suit.

He could still hear them laughing from two doors down. Hurrying to the refuge of the Men-Only Folly, he thought for the thousandth time that he'd never understand women.

FOURTEEN
SCANDAL

The facts are not in dispute; at precisely three forty-two on the Monday afternoon, four members of the rowing club were out on the lake. As they passed along the bank on the far side, they witnessed a scene so utterly astonishing, they could scarcely believe their eyes. Just visible among the thick shrub could be seen two heaving bodies very obviously engaged in an act of sexual intercourse. Without a doubt, what they saw was a female on her back, legs apart, accommodating a gentleman's bobbing buttocks. So shocked and disgusted were they by such animal behaviour that they immediately doubled back – as they said – just to make sure they hadn't been mistaken. Unfortunately for them, in the time it took to turn the boat around the errant pair had completed their business and scarpered.

As the rowers later testified, the scandalous incident occurred at about a quarter to four and by the time Alexander Armstrong was introducing *Pointless*, word had spread and there were few residents of Somerville Grange who hadn't heard the sensational news.

The witnesses were, of course, questioned at length, but

there was little reason not to believe them. After all, as stalwarts of the rowing club they were among the fittest in the community, not senile or gaga like some. And besides, all four had the same story to tell – and no, they had no idea who the couple might be, and no again, they could not identify them by what they were wearing because, as far as could be ascertained, they were both naked from the waist down.

Speculation was rife. Everyone had their own theory; any man with a roving eye came under suspicion and every woman who'd ever been thought of as mutton dressed as lamb was subject to speculative glances. Naturally, high among the suspects was Gloria Goodwood, the blonde bombshell of Somerville Grange, mainly because, for many of the men, she had featured in starring roles such as this in their own fantasies. But Gloria, along with the other members of the Am-Dram group, had cast-iron alibis; they were at the time rehearsing Gavin Madison's latest extravaganza in the old Ballroom.

Nor could any of Moira Muirfield's ladies have been involved, the simple reason being they were still beavering away at their handicrafts in the communal lounge at the time. But that didn't mean Moira didn't have something to say about the matter. Given that Miss Muirfield was a lady of impeccable character, it must surely have been an unfortunate slip of the tongue when she said that although she didn't know the lady involved, she thought she might be able to identify the male member.

It was a scattergun accusation which might have applied to any of the regulars in the male bastion in the Old Folly, a pack of reprobates who, in her opinion, she wouldn't trust as far as she could throw them. The news, of course, had been greeted in the club house with great hilarity and many a ribald comment, and if truth be told, more than a little envy.

Try though they may, no one at the Grange could come up with a positive identification of the lakeside lovers. Even the

Three Miss Marples were foxed, though, in fairness to them, the plots in Agatha Christie's stories were rarely spiced with as much naughtiness as this. Although, with three of them on the job, they might have come up with something.

Mostly, though, the reckoning was that one of the participants at least was married. This put a strain on several marriages, although one old fellow was secretly pleased that anyone might consider him sufficiently virile to be thought of as a latter-day Casanova.

In time, even the gossip-happy Grangers, unable to discover the truth of the matter, tired of the subject. There was, however, one person who knew the identity of the lakeside lovers but she was keeping her lips sealed. She it was who had given her married neighbour a book of short stories by Guy de Maupassant. In one of the stories, a couple are arrested and charged with fornication in a public place, having been discovered *in flagrante* among the bushes in a municipal park. On arrival at the police station, the authorities are amazed first of all to discover the couple to be well into their sixties and even more surprised that they had been married to each other for at least forty years. The reason for their indiscretion, they confessed, was that in all these years, they had never made love in the open air and they wanted to give it a go before it was too late. The simplest of explanations was that the incident at the lake at Somerville Grange was no more than a case of life imitating art.

By coincidence, the book the friend was currently reading was a turgid affair, with page after page of dreary social comment dragging down the narrative. Its saving grace, however, were the steamy passages describing in intimate detail several scenes of alfresco intercourse. But the friend had learned her lesson and, given her neighbour's reaction to the de Maupassant book, she had no intention of passing on her copy of *Lady Chatterley's Lover*.

FIFTEEN
THE EVACUEE

Gilly Mann was intrigued. A few days before she'd died, her friend and neighbour, Vera Welch, had given her a cheap and battered old trinket box.

'This is my treasure chest,' the old woman had confided. 'Don't open it till after I'm dead and buried.'

The burial had been that morning and, as they used to say in the old telly show, Gilly couldn't wait to open the box.

Over the years they'd been friendly, Gilly had frequently heard the romantic story of how Vera had been evacuated during the war to live with a family in an opulent villa on the outskirts of a small seaside town. The eight-year old child had been entranced by it, as the home she'd come from had been little more than a slum and never, even in her wildest dreams, could she have imagined that this would, in time, be the house where she would bring up her own children.

According to Vera, Harold, who became her husband, had little time for her during the war years, treating her with as much disdain as William Brown showed Violet Elizabeth Bott. It wasn't till years later that Harold was eventually smitten. As

Vera pertinently put it, 'Funny how a man's attitude changes when you develop a bust.'

Wondering what she might find in the shoddy casket, Gilly was disappointed to find it almost empty. The only item of note was an old diary tucked beneath a single lace glove, two wizened conkers and a collection of cigarette cards, part of an incomplete series of racing cars.

The diary was for the year 1941, written in a spidery, childish hand; not a day-to-day account but each entry spread over however many pages it took to complete whatever Vera had to say, irrespective of actual dates.

The first entry read: *This is a very nice house it is reely reely big. I like it here.*

Gilly was touched. She could just imagine how an eight-year-old girl might feel, transported from the confines of a poky city flat to an elegant detached villa, as splendid to her as a palace in a story book.

Turning the page, the next item puzzled Gilly. She'd never heard her friend talk about a boy called Sam; the son of the house, the one she'd eventually married, was called Harold.

I was at the beech today with Sam we padeled in the sea. I like Sam.

Almost every entry after that mentioned the adventures she shared with Sam. It was several pages in before Harold received any mention.

Harold was horid to Sam today I think he is jelos he nos I like Sam much more than Harold I love Sam.

Although Vera had never mentioned another son in the house, Gilly supposed Sam must have been Harold's younger brother, or even a boy from next door. Although later in the diary it becomes apparent that Sam lives in the big house, too. Gilly wondered if he might also have been an evacuee.

There followed page after page detailing the various adventures – a favourite word of Vera's – she shared with Sam. It seemed the pair were inseparable. Then suddenly, in the midst of all this carefree frolicking, came a passage so unbearably sad, Gilly's glasses misted up.

Bad news a bom has fell on our house and mum and dad are dead I reely shood be sad but it was a horid house and now mum and dad cant fite no more. Harold says I am a orfin.

The poor child! Gilly could barely imagine what it must have been like to be told you would never see your home or your parents again, and yet this chit of a girl appears to have taken it in her stride. Then again, perhaps this seeming heartlessness was the reason Vera hadn't wanted the diary to be read until after she'd died.

It seems to be winter when she writes again, a bitterly cold spell, when even the inside window ledges were iced in the morning. *It was reely cold last night but Sam came up in the midel of the night I cudeled him and we were nice and warm.*

Gilly was aghast. Even in wartime Britain it would surely have been wrong for an eight-year-old to share her bed with a member of the opposite sex. She was even more alarmed by the next entry.

I no its notty but Sam came up again last nite. Good old Sam.

Thankfully, there was no more mention of Sam's nocturnal visits; instead, the next page contained only one terse sentence.

Sam was poorly today.

Gilly had to stop at that point to answer the phone. When she opened the diary again, she was shaken by a totally unexpected revelation, a devastating statement blurred by childish teardrops.

Sam is dead.

Alone in her room, Gilly Mann was moved to tears herself, feeling the anguish her friend must have suffered all those years ago. An eight-year-old homeless orphan, who had now lost her greatest friend. Turning the page, Gilly braced herself for what might come next.

I hate the vet. The vet! Of course! She remembered now how much Vera loved dogs. She was especially fond of a particular mongrel collie. Perhaps it was a reincarnation of her faithful Sam. But how desolate Vera must have been in that dark midwinter when the world was at war. She was not to know then that, in the years to come, she would live a long and happy life, first of all with her husband and children in the wonderful house by the sea, followed by a contented decade in blissful retirement at Somerville Grange.

The room was in almost total darkness now. Switching on a light, Gilly turned to the final page of Vera's secret diary and the tears flowed again as she read the last poignant entry, written by a heartbroken child all those years ago.

I wos sad today so Harold bot me a ice creem.

SIXTEEN

CARROL AND CHRIS

C arrol and Chris were never referred to other than in the plural, two seemingly inseparable sisters, a cheery pair of chubby cherubs, their happy disposition guaranteed to bring instant smiles to the faces of friend and stranger alike. They'd both been widowed in the same year and had wisely decided to pool their resources and move to one of the attractive cottages at Somerville Grange.

In their years at The Grange, they'd become indispensable members of the social committee, ever eager to help with the organisation of communal events and, as valued members of the team, set up to welcome newcomers.

It was Carrol who noticed the feature in the local paper promoting a special gala night at a nearby hotel; a Cliff Richard-themed occasion with a tribute act performing hits made famous by the singer and his backing group, The Shadows. The sisters didn't often go out at night, but since they'd both been devoted fans of Cliff when they were young, they decided they'd make this exciting prospect an exception to that rule.

A taxi was arranged to take them to and from the venue and, after a great deal of deliberation on what they might wear, notwithstanding their fuller figures, they settled on sparkly tee shirts and tight blue jeans. With their hair drawn back in ponytails and wearing matching pairs of trendy trainers, looking for all the world like characters in a Beryl Cook painting, the sisters set out determined to enjoy a heady return to their teenage years.

Having led a sheltered life at The Grange, the sisters were unfamiliar with the concept of what is proudly proclaimed to be a "Tribute Act". This is usually a singer, or sometimes a group, pretending to be an established star or stars, cashing in on the original's success and saving themselves the trouble of having to develop a style of their own.

What they'd expected was some young fellow impersonating Cliff in his heyday. What they got instead was a performer closer in age to themselves, more a has-been idol than a teenage idol.

There was no visible backing group, only an ear-splitting backing track (why did it have to be so loud?) sounding nothing like The Shadows. Having booked the taxi to come for them at the end of the show, they had little option but to sit through the entire excruciating performance, aghast at the ludicrous notion that any Living Doll might be attracted to this old fraud.

Given the cost of the tickets and the expense of hiring a taxi, it had not been a cheap night; still, philosophical as ever, at least they were able to take one positive from the experience. If that old guy could get away with pretending to be a star performer, why couldn't they?

It just so happened, a couple of weeks later, that Gavin Madison, derivative as ever, was due to present his latest extravaganza, *Somerville has Talent*. Say what you like about the man, his name was box-office gold. You could be sure that if Gavin was involved with anything, it would be a guaranteed sell-out. There was, sad to say, a sadistic element in this enthusiasm, his avid fans wondering what disaster might next befall this master of ineptitude. This show. however, featuring the talented Grangers, proved to be an exception to the rule.

As expected, when the curtain opened on the first act, the old Ballroom was packed to overflowing. Among the audience was a group of the old guys who regularly frequented the Old Folly, the unofficial men's refuge. They'd come to give moral support to three of their number; Jim Curtis, Andrew Scott and Tommy Dale. From somewhere, Tommy had got hold of an old washboard, and Jim had a broom handle attached to a tea chest by a taut length of rope. Andrew, who had mastered the three basic chords on the guitar, led the trio in a rough and ready performance of skiffle hits made famous by Lonnie Donegan. The lads finished with *The Rock Island Line,* played at breakneck speed, earning them a warm round of applause, augmented by some ribald comments from their friends.

Determined to instil a measure of culture into the proceedings, Gavin had persuaded "Professor" Alexander Sinclair, the redoubtable brain of the Know-all's quiz team, to render the soliloquy from *Hamlet.* Looking every bit the part with his magnificent red beard, even the scallywags in the Old Folly gang were entranced by his dramatic delivery.

Keeping up the good work, the Three Miss Marples, Jane Douglas, Agnes Morrison and Mary Powell, all slant-eyed and saucy, sang *Three Little Maids* from *The Mikado.* This was followed by an unintentionally hilarious turn from the notoriously tone-deaf pianist, Elsie Blair, playing one of Winifred Atwell's boogie-woogie numbers in her own inimitable style.

Then for something completely different; the house lights dimmed and a single spot picked out the newcomer, Alice Nolan, demure and vulnerable, dressed in what her new-found partner, David Shaw, called her 'Sweet Little Alice Blue Gown'. Alice thrilled the hushed house with a plaintive, unaccompanied rendition of *Somewhere over the Rainbow,* her sweet, clear voice tugging at heartstrings and causing many a surreptitious tear. A fitting build-up to the final act.

Bounding on from one side of the stage came Peter Grant, a six-foot-six beanpole and from the other, the diminutive Charlie Cook, both dressed in fancy waistcoats and white bellbottom trousers. Then between them appeared the chubby sisters, Carrol and Chris, dolled out in mini-skirts and kinky boots, their irrepressible lust for life manifest in every elaborate step of the well-rehearsed choreography, as Little and Large and the two portly matrons mimed to recordings of *Abba's Greatest Hits*.

At the end, to rapturous applause, they were joined on stage by all the other featured acts, all of them a tribute to the indomitable spirit of the golden oldies at Somerville Grange, and an unexpected triumph for Gavin Madison.

SEVENTEEN

THE JULIET BALCONY

One of the windows in Edna March's flat had what is called a Juliet balcony; that is to say, when opened, there was a ledge about a foot or two deep, with a decorative iron rail. Hardly an adequate substitute for the real thing. When she'd first arrived at The Grange, it had scarcely registered among all the other new experiences. *Downsizing* was the word they used; they could say that again she thought. At first, she'd questioned the wisdom of moving into such a compact yet cosy flat, after years of living in a vast house which had once been home to herself, a husband, two sons, one daughter and, over the years, several dogs.

But now, more than a decade later, Edna had come to love the miniscule balcony. She'd been poorly for a while now and, unable to get out, spent much of her time at the open window, loving the warm sunshine and protected from any disruptive winds. It was, though, a reminder of just how much her world had shrunk. Once the virtual chatelaine of a demanding family home, time had left its mark; her husband Richard was the first to go, cruelly taken by cancer at an early age. Her two sons had long since flown the nest and only her daughter, Mary, visited regularly. She was expecting Mary that hot July afternoon.

Leaving the book she was reading open on her lap, Edna took comfort from the familiar view, the cluster of trees on the far side of the lake, an exuberance of midsummer greenery reflected on the placid water. From a carelessly opened window she heard a snatch of music, just enough to register before the window closed again. In that fleeting instant she recognised the tune, a song made popular in the 1950s by Frank Sinatra.

The memory took her back to her late teenage years, to the most magical time in her young life. She was on her first holiday without her parents, a week at Blackpool with her closest friend. She could remember as though it were yesterday the great sense of release, the rampant feeling of freedom, she'd felt that day; a chance to take on the world on her own terms. The afternoon had passed in careless abandon, bumping among the shrieking youngsters in the dodgem cars, tummy-tickling rides on chair-a-planes and heart-stopping thrills on the big dipper. Their faces burnt pink by exertion, salt air and the warm summer sun, they'd treated themselves to 99s, ice cream cones with a chocolate milk flake, a reckless extravagance by first-day-of-the-holiday millionaires.

Mingling with happy families freed from workaday worries, the girls strolled along the prom, loving the carnival atmosphere yet avoiding the temptation on offer from glitzy penny arcades and overtures from gipsy fortune tellers. They laughed in a superior way at the kiddies round the Punch and Judy show, but secretly wished they might still have been young enough to ride on the donkeys. Giddy with pleasure, they returned to their poky back-street digs for tea at five-o-clock. It had been a tidily-om-pom sort of day, beside the seaside, beside the sea.

Wonderful though the first day had been, the following afternoon was even better; ever after, Edna thought of this as her day of destiny. They'd gone to the world-famous Tower

Ballroom. Only recently restored after a devastating fire, for the two young girls it was an amazing experience to be in that most opulent of ballrooms. She could remember, even now, the heady sensation she'd felt then, the notion that adventure awaited and the intoxicating undercurrent of carnal expectation.

Magnificent chandeliers shone down on the multitude of dancers, the massed ranks ebbing and flowing in time to the music from the mighty Wurlitzer organ, played by Reginald Dixon, famous for his regular radio broadcasts on the Light Programme.

Sitting at her Juliet balcony, Edna could hear again the reedy strains of the old organ, playing the song that would become her favourite, *Around the World*. Her eyes closed and she was that eager, excited girl again, and suddenly Richard was there, not the emaciated husk she'd last seen in the pristine ghastliness of the hospice, but *her* Richard, young and virile. She could feel the rough tweed of his sports jacket, smell the Brylcreem on his hair. After all this time they were reunited, Edna and Richard, waltzing together once again in the Tower Ballroom.

Around the World thundered the organ and the young lovers swirled among the dancers, closer and closer. Then – fading – the sound of the organ grew more distant, echoing and discordant, and a single tear ran down the old woman's cheek and the book fell from her lap.

'Mother!' called Mary, letting herself in. 'Sorry I'm late.' Then 'Mother?' again, this time anxiously.

An ambulance was called but there was nothing they could do.

EIGHTEEN
THE SECOND TIME AROUND

Here at last was something the Three Miss Marples, Agnes Morrison, Jane Douglas and Mary Powell, could get their teeth into. The three elderly ladies, who rather fancied themselves as latter-day detectives in the mould of Agatha Christie's well-loved character had, thanks to their "little treasure", Tanya Miller, learned about the forthcoming marriage of two employees at the Grange, Anna Turpin and Daniel Cope.

What interested the ladies was the back story to this romance. Both the prospective bride and her groom worked at the retirement complex; Anna in the residents' restaurant and Daniel with the hard-working team of gardeners. Most of the workers at the Grange came from the local village, just as in days of yore the Big House had employed local lads and lassies. But in this case the coincidence went even further, as some of the older folk in the village had a vague notion that there had been a wedding between two villagers who had also been employed at "Up There" around the time of the Great War, and they too had been called Anna Turpin and Daniel Cope.

'How very exciting!' exclaimed Agnes Morrison.

'It's déjà vu all over again,' gushed Jane Douglas.

Mary Powell, who was a great fan of the programme *Who Do You Think You Are?*, had a more constructive reaction. 'Well, what's stopping us? Let's check out the parish records.'

The following day, the three redoubtable ladies arrived as arranged, at two o'clock in St Peter's, the local church. Twenty minutes later, a grumpy jobsworth, complaining all the while, let them into the vestry and unceremoniously dumped an ancient tome on the table. He then informed them he would return within the hour, by which time he hoped they would have concluded their business and he could get back to the comfort of his own home.

Quite put out by the man's appalling manners, it was only after he'd gone they discovered the parish records in the book he'd given them took them only to the end of the nineteenth century. An inconvenience to be sure, but here was a chance to do some real detective work. They could at least check the approximate dates of birth, to see if any matched the original Anna and Daniel.

Turpin and Cope, they soon discovered, were the surnames of well-established families in the area. The Copes, they noted with interest, had originally been refugees from Hungary, the new name an Anglified version of Kopocek, or some such. Two entries, one for a boy born in 1896 and the other for a girl in 1898, rewarded their enterprise. The names matched and they would both have been about the right age to be married at the time of The Great War.

As they were congratulating themselves on their good work, the curmudgeon returned, as ill-mannered as ever, snatched the book and packed it away, saying 'Time up, ladies, time to go home.'

'I don't think so,' said Mary, speaking quietly and deliberately. 'We still have to check out the record of marriages at the time of the First World War.'

At that moment, the nasty official realised he'd made two big mistakes. In the first instance, he'd seriously underestimated the resolve of the elderly ladies and, secondly, he'd left his keys lying on the table.

Jane locked the door, preventing his escape, Agnes reminded him in no uncertain terms which volume they now required and Mary toyed menacingly with her umbrella. Cowed into compliance, the odious man did as he was asked. After that, it didn't take long to find the information they sought. Anna Turpin and Daniel Cope had indeed been wed in St Peter's, on the second of May 1916.

As they left the church, feeling well pleased with themselves, they were passing the War Memorial when Agnes Morrison stopped short. There among the names of the fallen were the names of two Copes, one of them called Thomas, the other Daniel. Surely not? If that was the same Daniel, it would mean Anna would have been widowed within two years.

The regimental records were consulted, with the tragic revelation that it was indeed the same Daniel. His company had embarked for France on the third of May, 1916, the day after his wedding. On the first of July that year, Daniel and almost twenty thousand other British soldiers lost their lives on the disastrous First Day on the Somme. The heart-breaking truth of the matter was that the original Anna and Daniel were together as a married couple for only one night.

That was the bad news. The good news was that the Grangers were so taken by the sad story that the young couple received a generous cash gift, allowing them to make up the shortfall and put down a deposit on one of the "affordable houses" being built in the village.

And so, more than a hundred years after their ill-fated predecessors, in the same small village church, Anna Turpin and Daniel Cope were joined together in holy matrimony. Prominent among the packed congregation, wearing show-stopping hats, were Agnes Morrison, Jane Douglas and Mary Powell, the Three Miss Marples.

NINETEEN
THE NOISY NEIGHBOURS

The talk that morning in the Old Folly, the regular refuge for male residents seeking an escape from scolding wives or predatory widows, was all about a newcomer who had been reprimanded for disturbing the peace of his neighbours. It turned out he wasn't deaf, as they'd imagined, but just liked to play his music at top volume. A visit from the social committee soon put a stop to such thoughtless behaviour, and the other residents were once more able to enjoy the peace and serenity to be expected in such an exclusive and expensive retreat.

If only it had been as easy back then, thought Tommy Dale, remembering the blighted year when he and his then neighbours had suffered the daily torment from a family of belligerent newcomers who cared little or nothing about the sensitivities of others. All that summer, insufferably loud rock music blasted from the offending house. Polite requests to turn it down a bit were met with contempt, or even with an increase in the volume.

The Preston family, Ma, Pa and delinquent son, were an unruly lot. Not only did they outrage the neighbours with their intrusive music, but Preston Junior regularly endangered life and limb, driving his souped-up Ford Escort at irresponsibly high speed along the narrow, tree-lined avenues. Rough-spoken and profane, the family's behaviour fell far short of what might be expected in a respectable des-res suburb. 'More like Mean Street, USA,' grumbled one irate resident.

One afternoon, Tommy had been out on his patio. The sun was shining, but relaxation was impossible due to the mind-numbing persistence of a throbbing bass guitar. Unable to concentrate on the magazine article he was trying to read, he flicked to the back pages and came across an arresting advertisement for a grandfather clock. 'Send no money now,' it illogically stated. 'If not completely satisfied, item can be returned within ten days.' He smiled at that, imagining the reception he'd get from the sour-faced sub-post mistress, confronted with such a request. And that was when, as his grandchildren would say, he had his light bulb moment.

Abandoning his recliner, Tommy took a stroll round the block, ascertained the Preston's address, and, by a stroke of good luck, the telephone number, too. Preston the younger had his hot-rod car up for sale with home contact details prominently displayed. Bingo!

Over the course of the next few days, the anti-social Preston family received not only a grandfather clock, but a thirty-piece dinner set, twelve leather-bound volumes of *Encyclopaedia Britannica* and an upmarket petrol driven lawnmower. In addition, they were visited by double glazing salesmen, representatives from home improvement services and optimistic landscape gardeners, all under the impression the Prestons had requested quotations. Tommy was unrelenting in his research, sending the Prestons' details to each and every advertised service or unmissable offer requiring only a name, address and phone number.

In passing, it should perhaps be mentioned that, when telling this story to his grandchildren, Tommy had to explain that in the days before on-line shopping, it was common practice for advertisers to offer their merchandise with deferred payment. In the same way as in these prehistoric times, one landline telephone number was shared by the entire family.

As the summer progressed, if ever Tommy had any qualms about his crude campaign, an afternoon spent on his decibel-blasted patio convinced him the Prestons deserved all the angst he could conjure up – and more.

Eventually, the warm summer turned into autumn, the days grew shorter, life returned indoors and the disruptive behaviour from the Preston household affected only their immediate neighbours. Around this time, Jenny Hardcastle, a notorious curtain-twitcher who lived opposite the Prestons, gave Tommy a ringside account of recent events concerning the disruptive family. Just as Tommy had imagined, the sub-post mistress had refused to accept any more return parcels and there had been a number of acrimonious exchanges with disappointed salesmen.

Happy to have caused the Prestons so much inconvenience, Tommy enjoyed the relative quiet of the winter days, but still dreaded the prospect of another ruined summer. He needn't have worried. His cunning enterprise seemed to have been rewarded. Jenny Hardcastle contacted him with the welcome news; a *For Sale* sign had appeared in the Prestons' front garden and before the clocks were changed, the anti-social family had gone.

Tommy Dale was a modest man and of course he would never know for certain if he had been directly responsible for the Preston family's hasty departure. However, reprehensible as some might think his behaviour, if ever faced with a similar challenge, he would happily resort to the same extreme methods. Thankfully, that would be unlikely in the civilised surroundings of Somerville Grange.

TWENTY

HAPPENSTANCE

3 *across. A coincidence for Uncle Sam (12).*
Anita Longstaff laughed out loud. Just by chance, only that afternoon at the book-reading club they'd been discussing American words and expressions now commonplace in written English, among them, "upcoming" for "forthcoming", "to grow", in place of "to develop" and, wouldn't you just know, "happenstance" for "coincidence".

Casting the crossword aside, she thought about the subtle difference between the two words and how, in the course of her life, she'd been the victim of a cruel Anglo-Saxon coincidence and the beneficiary of one happy Yankee-doodle happenstance.

She was in her early thirties when, one stormy night, an ancient oak tree which had stood on the same spot for countless years, chose the very moment her husband Bill was driving past to collapse, crushing car and driver.

Widowed at a ridiculously young age and with a sullen sub-teenage daughter to contend with, it had been the most trying time of her life. She was still relatively young and knew, sooner or later, she'd have to get out a bit more, but her heart just wasn't in it. Until, that is, she was called for jury duty.

In her despondent state, Anita was further depressed by the sordid details of the trial. But all that changed when the main witness for the prosecution was called. Introduced as the arresting officer, he immediately captured Anita's attention. For the first time since the tragic accident, Anita experienced a genuine spark of attraction.

After the trial, she couldn't get him out of her mind. The romantic notions lifted her spirits considerably, winning over the guilty thought that she was being disloyal to her not-so-late husband with her girlish infatuation – that is, until she remembered the numerous occasions Bill had candidly admitted that if ever the opportunity presented itself, he would gladly have run off with Brit Ekland. Goose and gander sauce in different bottles. Made no matter, anyway. Chance would be a fine thing and there was no harm in dreaming.

On a Sunday afternoon a couple of weeks after the court case, she was walking in the park. Although since the trial, for whatever reason, she'd recovered some of her former vitality, the sight of happy, seemingly carefree families reminded her of other Sundays she'd enjoyed with Bill and their then more biddable daughter.

As she approached the ornamental pond with its broad promenade, her path was blocked by a selfish group of gossiping dog-walkers and unruly children. She would normally have walked round in a clockwise direction, but because of this human and canine obstruction, she was obliged on this occasion, against her will, to go the other way.

She was on the long, straight stretch when she saw *him* in the distance, walking towards her. For a second, she thought it might just be wishful thinking, but as he came closer it became certain it really was the officer from the trial. In a moment, he would have been past and out of her life forever, but then, just as he drew level, he stopped in his tracks. Looking in her direction with a frown of hesitant recognition, almost apologetically he asked, 'Hey! Didn't I see you in court?'

'Guilty as charged, your honour,' Anita simpered, instinctively coy and flirtatious, making him laugh.

'My name's James, I was the police officer in the case.'

'Pleased to meetya, James,' all doe-eyed and goofy now, 'I'm Anita. You wanna take down my particulars?'

It was a great start and they never looked back. Although they didn't marry, Anita and James were together constantly until parted by death. And of course, happenstance had played its part, for if Anita's normal route round the pond hadn't been blocked by the gossiping families and their dogs, she would have been walking behind James on that fateful Sunday and their paths might never have crossed.

Anita picked up the crossword again, filled in the answer to 3 across, then smiled, remembering how The Grange's erudite "Professor" Alexander Sinclair had summed up the discussion at the book-club that afternoon: 'Coincidence or happenstance, makes no difference,' he said. 'What's for you won't go past you, it's just your Donald Duck.'

TWENTY-ONE
WALK THIS WAY

The expression, "Living the Dream", although probably transatlantic in origin, could have been coined with just such a heavenly setting as Somerville Grange in mind. That the fortunate residents should have had to wait until the bell rang at the beginning of the last lap before availing themselves of the delights and comfort on offer there, only made it all the more precious. And no one appreciated the good luck that allowed him the chance to pass his remaining days in such splendid surroundings more that Jim Curtis.

Jim, as they might have said when he was young, had come from humble beginnings; his parents, had they still been alive, would have been amazed by their offspring's casual affluence. Never a day dawned but Jim gave thanks for the way his personal cookie had crumbled. It was the simple things he appreciated most; like opening his curtains in the morning and looking out across the lake to the distant forest, thrilled by the constant contrast of the changing colours, season by season.

No matter the time of year, Jim delighted in exploring the extensive grounds, once the preserve of a privileged few. His favourite walk took in the understated splendour of the walled garden, loving the extravagant flourish of the Japanese blossoms in the spring, savouring the successive delights of azaleas, rhododendrons and other exotic blooms as the summer progressed. Even in the dark, dead days of winter, there was comfort to be taken from the resolute defiance of the frost-bound trees, patiently awaiting the warmer days to come.

Other times, when he was feeling most active, he would follow the path which led past the walled garden, taking in the grand sweep of the manicured lawn with, at the far end, the fiendishly tricky crazy-golf course, with picturesque windmills and cunning tunnels among the testing and intricate hazards. It was a feature popular with the former golfers among the residents, who were no longer up to the real thing but relished the opportunity to exercise the skills learned over a lifetime misspent on lush courses and windswept links.

Beyond the putting area, the path winds downward then joins the wider walkway round the lake, the popular promenade favoured on fine days by gregarious Grangers, there to meet and greet, gracious as to the manner born.

Around the curve of the lake stands a small boathouse, a modest housing for the collection of rowing boats, an amenity installed in years gone by at the whim of a fanciful member of the Forsyth family, little imagining how popular in time the boats might become among the more energetic Grangers. The enthusiasts in the model-boat club meet here, too; the stout jetty providing the ideal launch site for their replica destroyers and full-rigged sailing-ships, many of them constructed in minute and loving detail by the members themselves. Just don't get them started on the finer points of the process.

Once or twice a year, when the mood took him, Jim would cut through the forest on the other side of the lake, forever fascinated by the remains of a once substantial dry-stone dyke on the far periphery of the wood. Smothered in bracken and brier, the wall, built perhaps when Victoria was on the throne or even earlier, forsaken and forgotten now, must once have had some purpose.

Jim tried to imagine the skilled craftsman who built this wall; he thought of him as Tam, a wizened worthy, out in all weathers, a master of his craft earning but a pittance. Here was a man of his time, content with his lot, a man probably well thought of in the community, never imagining that working men could ever aspire to anything beyond a life of servitude. Never in his wildest dreams could Tam have imagined that Somerville Grange would one day be tenanted by men and women from the common herd, low-born folks like himself.

As ever when his thoughts ran this way, Jim marvelled anew at his own good fortune, to have been born in more enlightened times, to have been given the chance to forge his own destiny.

On his return journey, he joined the cinder track known as the "back path", which ran from the lake past the eccentric delight of the crenulated folly, once the setting for elite garden parties in bygone times, now the preserve of the gentlemen residents, replete with super-sized television screen.

On the last lap now, as Jim approached the original manor house, he would often pause to appreciate the understated splendour of the old building, tastefully adapted to its present use. If a stranger was unaware of its present incarnation as an elite retirement complex, he might well imagine this to be the well-preserved home of some noble family. From outside, it was impossible to tell the ancient house was now host to a score of well-appointed flats; that the dining room was a popular restaurant, as chic as any West End bistro and the main drawing room served as an ultra-superior sewing room, a meeting place for the Grange's womenfolk, renowned for nimble needle-work and wagging tongues.

Off to the left of the impressive entrance hallway lies the beating heart of Somerville Grange; the former ballroom, adapted now as an all-purpose function room, hosting sedate tea dances, community council meetings, concerts and – the icing on the cake – the ever-popular shows staged by Gavin Madison and his am-dram enthusiasts.

Less than fifty yards from the main building, Jim completed his circuit, returning to his own flat in one of the impressive blocks dotted about the grounds, each housing a dozen or more individual units, cunningly designed to look like impressive villas, no two alike.

Jim Curtis was not a religious man, but never a day passed that he didn't give thanks to whatever form of fate had decreed that he should end his days in such an earthly paradise. Like a character in a fairy-tale, he was living happily ever after; living the dream at Somerville Grange.

TWENTY-TWO
THE CELEBRITY

'What's the difference between vegan and vegetarian?' asked plump-as-a-dumpling Carrol of her equally well upholstered sister, Chris. Not that they were thinking of a drastic alteration of their eating habits; they'd managed quite well, thank you, on a regular diet of puddings and pies and saw no reason to forgo these earthly pleasures for any passing fad. No, the reason this question was being asked that morning in kitchens all over Somerville Grange was in response to Gavin Madison's latest wheeze.

Gavin, the Grange's irrepressible entertainment guru, had the previous day sought entrants for yet another cooking competition; this time, the quest was for the person who could come up with the most appetising vegan main meal. As a special inducement – since the Grangers were well used to Gavin's madcap projects – it was intimated that the contest would be graced by a celebrity judge.

Who, wondered the Grangers, might this mysterious celebrity be? The ladies, busy with their handicrafts, could talk of nothing else and the subject was even discussed among the menfolk in the Old Folly; for a while at least, Premier League action took second place to speculation as to the identity of the promised celebrity.

Given his track record, no one should have been surprised when Gavin Madison eventually disclosed the identity of the star attraction. Although only a certifiable optimist would have expected Gavin to have procured the services of, say, Mary Berry, or Carol Vorderman, they hadn't expected anyone quite as underwhelming as Sissie Snodgrass.

Quite how one attains celebrity status is a much-debated subject. Discounting actual film stars, cast members of long running soaps and a handful of international sports personalities, it seems there is a substantial substrata of second and third rate personalities, promoted beyond their abilities, such as participants in unrealistic "reality shows", once-famous pop stars and pious green activists. Taking up the rear, there are others who, by chance, happened to catch the passing moment. Sissie Snodgrass was just such a one.

Few people had heard of her before she made several appearances on local television news bulletins in a long-running feud about an invasive Leylandii hedge. Austin Breen, a small-time variety agent, was sufficiently impressed to take her on his books and, as he said, she'd never looked back. Her CV listed the opening of a poodle parlour, a gig turning on the Christmas lights in a small village and presenting the prizes at the school spelling bee in the same small village

In not quite a lather of excitement, the Grangers gathered round the poster advertising the contest, featuring a promotional photo of the mysterious celebrity. What they saw was a fifty-something, with what would once have been described as an hourglass figure, topped by a bubble of fizzy blue hair, peering panda-eyed towards the camera. An image airily dismissed by Moira Muirfield. 'Sissie Snodgrass,' she snorted, 'not to be confused with Barbara Cartland.'

Come the big day, before a sparse assembly in the former

ballroom, the contestants lined up behind their occasionally burnt offerings. Reading from left to right; relative newcomer Alice Nolan, the tubby sisters Chris and Carrol, each with her own concoction. Then came Noel Davidson as the token male entrant, Else Blair, the notoriously tone-deaf pianist and, almost out of sight, the wee woman whose name no-one could ever remember.

Obviously in thrall to her own publicity, Sissy Snodgrass made a great show of sampling the entries. For the already bored audience, this process, lacking televised close-ups or witty commentary, matched only the process of drying paint for excitement. Eventually, all coy sweetness and condescension, imagining herself addressing millions of rapt viewers, she turned to the dozing Grangers, treating them to a right-on lecture about the importance of vegan and vegetarian values in the effort to save our planet, supported – she modestly inferred – by many other celebrities like herself. Finally, after waffling on in this manner for what seemed to the contestants, who were obliged to stay standing through-out, like an eternity, she at last got down to the business in hand.

'It therefore gives me great pleasure to announce that the winner is… ' Then, in time-honoured fashion, she paused, the sudden silence startling some of the audience to wakefulness, only just in time to witness the most dramatic moment of the afternoon. Before she could utter another word, Sissy Snodgrass collapsed as though mortally stricken, before being dragged unceremoniously into the wings by a panic-stricken Gavin Madison.

They never found out who the winner was, just as they never found out which particular ingredient from the vegan concoctions caused the devastating attack of food poising which had so spectacularly felled Sissy Snodgrass. Fortunately, Sissy's health recovered but alas, she was dropped by her agent, Austin

Breen and, other than by her relatives and close friends, was never heard of again.

As recompense for their involvement in the culinary fiasco, Gavin Madison treated the contestants to a meal the following weekend in the Residents' Restaurant. There, hale and hearty, unlike the unfortunate judge, they tucked into a traditional Sunday roast.

TWENTY-THREE

HECTOR WAINWRIGHT

When, almost a decade ago, Hector Wainwright moved into Somerville Grange, his first task was to replace the solid, outdated and outsized furniture from the gloomy old house he'd lived in for most of his life. The only item he retained was the sturdy writing bureau which had belonged to his father. Staunch as the oak from which it was fashioned, this magnificent desk had been the launching pad for countless letters to newspapers, periodicals and even, occasionally, to cabinet ministers who might have found themselves at odds with old Archibald Wainwright, and his intractable opinions.

After his father's death, Hector carried on the family tradition. He treasured the majestic writing bureau, loving the intricacy of its design, the multitude of finely crafted drawers and pigeon-holes. Most of all, he loved the moment when he lowered the front of the cabinet and the green writing surface was revealed. He savoured the sensuous pleasure to be had by simply drawing a virgin sheet from the alcove, ready to draft another faultlessly calligraphed letter, to whomsoever it may concern.

Soon after he moved to Somerville Grange, however, it

slowly dawned on Hector that times had changed. It was no longer a case of letters to the editor; now, the published items were more often delivered by e-mail. Unwilling to compromise, Hector soldiered on, dashing off his usual volume of perfectly presented communications, but with a diminishing return to show for his efforts. All too often, by the time his contributions arrived by snail mail, the correspondence had moved on or had even been discontinued.

Not completely disheartened, Hector carried on, but now focusing on monthly magazines with a more leisurely turnover of topics. It was one of his letters to just such a publication which inadvertently changed his life for ever.

In his usual bombastic fashion, Hector pointed out a number of anachronisms in a recently televised period drama and had the satisfaction of having the letter published, just another success to add to a long list. He'd thought no more about it until, a week or so later, a letter arrived, tentatively concurring with every point he'd made. The writer hoped he wouldn't mind her contacting him at his home address, but she wanted him to know she was in complete agreement with all he'd said.

Hector read the letter several times over. It was, of course, flattering that anyone would take the trouble to write to him personally, but what impressed him most was the impeccable handwriting, a handsome copperplate as precise and correct as his own.

For a short time, long ago, Hector had been unhappily married. Too late, his young wife discovered she'd married one of nature's bachelors. Quickly tiring of his prissy ways, she'd sent him packing back to his widower father's gloomy house. Since then, there had been no other woman in his life, but he was immediately attracted to this unexpected female correspondent. Over the next five years, they exchanged letters at least twice a week, confirming an uncannily harmonious outlook on the world. Here, it seemed, late in life, in the letters from Effie McDade writing from the Kingdom of Fife, Hector Wainwright had found a kindred spirit.

Strangely, in all that time they never proposed a meeting, nor did they exchange photographs. Hector was, for his part, happy to imagine Effie as the epitome of every man's perfect woman; a female version of himself.

Over the years, they discussed every topic under the sun, joyfully finding common ground in politics, entertainment and the arts, but communicating very little of a personal nature. Effie didn't mention the cancer until her very last letter.

Hector was devastated. How, he wondered, could he cope without Effie's regular communications? "Closure" was too modern a concept to have made much impression on a dry old stick like Hector Wainwright, but instinctively he felt the need to visit the small fishing village on the east coast of Scotland, as a mark of respect to the woman who had become his virtual soul mate.

The house that once belonged to Effie McDade stood amid a long row of fishermen's cottages, overlooking the quaint old harbour. An empty house now, the curtainless windows staring blind-eyed across a pathetically small garden. Sitting at a table by the window in a cosy and convenient tea-room, Hector, full of sadness and recrimination, watched as a Salvation Army van drew up outside Effie's house. A pair of hefty chaps started moving out furniture from the house and into the van. They made a couple of trips before they brought out an item, the sight of which left Hector stunned and open-mouthed.

Huffing and puffing, they carefully manoeuvred the object out the small doorway. It was an elaborate writing bureau, identical in every respect to his own cherished heirloom.

A kindred spirit indeed.

TWENTY-FOUR
A RAY OF SUNSHINE

As you might expect, given that Somerville Grange is the domain of fortunate old-timers enjoying the delights of the exclusive retirement complex, it goes without saying that a three-year-old child in their midst would be the source of much debate. All the more so if that same child had several distinctive characteristics.

If they were being honest, some might have harboured old-fashioned attitudes about racial prejudice, while others might simply have objected to having any child about the place. That, though, would have been before any of them had seen her.

'A positive ray of sunshine!' declared Gloria Goodwood, delighting in the child's beaming smile, charmed by her mischievous brown eyes and impressed beyond measure by her sassy self-regard; never for a minute thinking anyone could be other than charmed by such lovable little minx as herself. 'An absolute poppet,' enthused Gloria.

The Grangers, however, were presented with a dilemma; should they describe the child as black, or coloured? Apparently one term was acceptable now, the other not, but no one was sure just which one.

The child's name was Elisa, the granddaughter of Alice Nolan. She was in Alice's keeping for a week to allow Elisa's mother and her West Indian father, who had only recently married, to enjoy a honeymoon without the distraction of a three-year-old. Hearing this, some of the older women, whose wedding dresses on their big day had been a little too tight for comfort, remarked at how much things had changed since their young day.

Elisa soon made her presence felt. A curious child with few inhibitions, she was likely to pop up anywhere, often uninvited but always welcomed, even venturing into the male preserve in the Old Folly. There, she took a fancy to Alexander Sinclair, or at least to his bristling red beard, sitting on the arm of his chair, grabbing handfuls in her tiny fists and giggling at his affected outrage. The "Professor" would have dearly loved to give her a hug, but even in the presence of a dozen others, to do so might lay him open to accusations of inappropriate behaviour. What, he wondered, had the world come to?

Elisa's favourite port of call was the home of sisters, Chris and Carrol, 'The two fat ladies,' as Eliza called them with disarming frankness. To see the tubby sisters and the doll-like toddler together was as if one of Lucy Atwell's cherubic cuties – albeit several shades darker – had wandered into a painting by Beryl Cook; and if that didn't bring a smile to your face, nothing ever would.

The sisters were enchanted by their tiny guest, delighting in her impromptu song and dance routines, reminding them of Shirley Temple in the films when they were young. Elisa's favourite song was *You Are My Sunshine*, and that's what prompted Chris and Carrol to get in touch with Gavin Madison.

The much-maligned Gavin had, some time ago, instituted a series of Sunday concerts featuring a local ukulele orchestra. The Grangers loved them, infected by the enthusiasm and the obvious delight the performers took in their simple music-making.

In the week that the Grange was honoured by the visit of young Elisa, the Sunday was warm and sunny and the concert was given on the lawn before the Big House. As ever, the Grangers joined in the singing of the popular songs, old and new, thoroughly enjoying their afternoon entertainment, little knowing the best was yet to come.

Gavin Maddison, at the behest of Chris and Carrol had, the previous day, arranged a secret rehearsal with the orchestra leader. As a result, almost at the end of the concert, a little girl dressed in denim dungarees, her fuzzy hair controlled in two sticky-out bunches and with all the aplomb of seasoned diva, strode nonchalantly on to the stage. Backed by the harmonious plonk of a score of ukuleles, the tiny tot sang her heart out, earning a standing ovation and cries of 'Encore!' from her misty-eyed audience.

A few days later, all too soon, Elisa's stay at Somerville Grange was over and her mother returned to reclaim her adorable daughter, leaving the Grangers bereft; she had taken their sunshine away.

TWENTY-FIVE
HIS OLD FLAME

Of course Ben Wilson was aware of Eileen Grey's arrival at Somerville Grange, it was a major talking point in the Old Folly. The old chaps who congregated there, as was their wont, had taken only one look at this well-preserved beauty and awarded the newcomer a rating of nine out of ten. Just how this spectacular total was arrived at is perhaps best left to conjecture; suffice to say, no matter how old they are, boys will always be boys.

Although he'd seen the new arrival from afar, it wasn't until he was lunching in the Residents' Restaurant with two of his cronies that Ben realised their paths had crossed before. Eileen was at an adjacent table with the Grange's other notable beauty, Gloria Goodwood; perhaps it was a casual gesture or a trill of laughter, but suddenly he realised he'd know her in the dim and distant past.

'Eileen Howard!' he exclaimed, startling his dining companions and even himself with his impetuosity. A pair of alarmed but exquisite blue eyes regarded him quizzically. 'We went to the same school. You were Eileen Howard then,' Ben stumbled on, ' and I was – or rather I still am – Ben Wilson.'

There was an embarrassed silence, diners and staff engrossed in the sudden drama. Then, her exquisite features lit by a happy smile of recognition, Eileen replied, 'Of course, of course! How sweet of you to remember me after all these years.'

The tension relaxed and the mood changed, helped by Gloria's melodramatic intervention. 'How absolutely marvellous, my dear. Who would have thought you'd come across an old flame at Somerville Grange?'

Happy to be the centre of attention, Eileen did nothing to play down the fairytale nature of the unlikely reunion. The ladies in the community were enthralled. Ben Wilson was still a handsome man and he and Eileen seemed made for each other. The unreformed misogynists in the Old Folly had much the same opinion, though expressed somewhat differently, along the lines of, 'Get in there, my son.'

The only person not at ease with the situation was Ben himself. To be considered an old flame was, as he saw it, pitching it a bit high. Their great romance had consisted of nothing more than a solitary date, a visit to the local picture house. Of course they'd kissed and cuddled and he'd fondled her breasts, but that was par for the course in those days. What he most remembered about their big night out was that it had cost him ten bob, a princely sum back then. He'd been skint for the rest of the week.

Although in the intervening years Ben had proved himself a shrewd operator in the money markets, proof positive being that he could easily afford the upkeep of one of the better cottages at Somerville Grange, he would be first to agree he was no Casanova, and the prospect of entering into a sexual relationship with the delectable Eileen filled him with dread.

Throughout his marriage, he had been faithful to his late wife and no enticing opportunities had come his way since. Furthermore, he was alarmed by articles he'd read about what was expected from gentlemen in that department nowadays.

Modern women, it seemed, expected great sex. What on earth constituted great sex? Even the expression, 'sexually active women,' conjured up a picture of athletic Amazons, slinking into the bedroom in skimpy undies, demanding attention. To add to his concerns, he learned that Eileen had been thrice married and would obviously have had much more experience in these matter than himself. It was a daunting prospect.

He needn't have worried. When the time came, Eileen did indeed turn out to be an able lover. An experienced woman who knew just what she wanted from her men and how to get it. With an erotic mix of tenderness and guile, she soon banished his inhibitions, to their mutual satisfaction.

A few weeks later, toddling home after one of their regular trysts, Ben reflected that the ten bob he'd splashed out in a trip to the flicks all these years ago, had turned into quite the best investment he'd ever made.

TWENTY-SIX

CHRISTMAS EVE

Despite the promise of idyllic snowy landscapes on festive greeting cards, Christmas Eve seldom lives up to its billing. Falling as it does in the bleak midwinter, it's more often damp and dismal with treacherous conditions underfoot. Christmas may be a magical time for children, but for the oldies at Somerville Grange, wearied by the long commercial slog leading up to the great day, it also brings poignant thoughts of Christmases past, memories of times gone by, as the old song has it, when joy and sadness mingle.

Over the years, a tradition has developed at the Grange; the residents, well muffled, congregate in the former ballroom around five o'clock on Christmas Eve, in time for the annual broadcast of carols from King's College Cambridge. Shown on the giant screen in the darkened room, they can easily persuade themselves that they are actually present in the ancient chapel. It is an eagerly awaited occasion and an important date in the Grangers' social calendar.

Later than she had intended, the nice wee woman whose name no-one could ever remember, excusing herself and nodding shyly as she squeezed along the row, slipped into a seat near the back of the hall. She was only just in time; the sweet, pure voice of the chosen chorister stilled any chatter, the audience instantly beguiled. 'Once in royal David's City,' he sang and the hour of magic was underway.

Like many another at that time of year, she thought back longingly to her earliest Christmas memories. She remembered being carried, still sleepy-eyed, in her father's arms to open the presents Santa Claus had magically delivered in the night. It was a pitiful collection by today's standards. Her main present that year, one she would cherish for years to come, was the red Tam o' Shanter, like the one Margaret O'Brian had worn in a recent film. Tucked away at the bottom of her stocking was the obligatory orange, the sixpenny piece, and a slim bar of wartime chocolate. Propped against the tree was yet another treasure; her very first Rupert Bear annual.

She would never forget that wonderful morning. Sometimes even now, she imagined she could smell again the musky masculine tang of her father, the only man there had ever been in her life. Like so many fathers in the twentieth century, he went off to war and never returned.

Hers had been a lonely childhood, brought up in a repressive household by her war-widowed mother and her mother's unmarried sister. In thrall to the dictates of a mean-spirited religious sect, she was discouraged from making friends with her sinful schoolmates.

When she was young, she'd taken refuge in her imagination. Her friends were the inhabitants of Nutwood, the home of Rupert Bear in the stories in her prized collection of annuals. During the many years she skivvied in the dim and dismal family home, looking after her mother and her aunt, she'd dreamed that someday she would escape to just such a place as Nutwood.

By the time her mother, soon after the demise of her aunt, followed her sister to the Spartan heaven they'd been promised by the holier-than-thou preachers, the wee woman, now in her sixties, seized her chance. Quite serendipitously, a few months before she'd been set free, a brochure came through the post advertising the delights of Somerville Grange. One speculative visit and her mind had been made up and, with indecent but understandable haste, she'd sold up the gloomy old family home and moved into her very own version of Nutwood.

Between the carols relayed to the old ballroom there were readings from the King James Bible, the majestic prose so unlike the turgid story-book version favoured by the pastors at the Gospel Hall. Small wonder, she thought, that church-going was in decline; with all that mealy-mouthed cant along the way, the scriptures had lost their mystique.

Towards the end of the service, the Grangers joined in, singing with lusty conviction the final joyful anthem, *Hark The Herald Angels Sing*. It brought angry tears of regret to the wee woman's eyes, as she remembered a lifetime of un-festive Christmas Eves with her mother and her aunt among the narrow-minded bigots.

It was dark, wet and windy as the Grangers filed out, huddled against the cold, anxious to regain the comfort of their cosy homes. The wee woman whose name no-one could remember was thrilled be to be wished a merry Christmas by so many of her neighbours, though none of them addressed her by name. She had long since come to terms with her anonymous standing and now, as never before, she found contentment at the Grange, her only regret being that she hadn't been able to make the move sooner.

TWENTY-SEVEN

FROM DAWN TO DUSK

The sun was only just coming up when Tommy Dale, who had risen half-an-hour earlier, collected the batch of morning newspapers deposited in the reception area by the local newsagent. As a favour, Tommy, who was an early riser, was happy to be up and about making deliveries to stay-a-bed Grangers, still set in their ways, who liked to peruse the daily news from the printed page.

In his far-off youth, like many another boy of his generation, Tommy had had an early morning paper run and, by obliging the Grangers in this way, he could indulge in the illusion that he was still the spritely lad he'd been all those years ago. The only concession he made to old age was his refusal to deliver on Saturdays and Sundays when, as he often remarked, a pack horse would be needed to carry the outrageous quantity of supplements and advertising inserts in the weekend press.

Thanks to Tommy, when the tubby sisters, Carrol and Chris, sat down to their substantial breakfast about eight o'clock, the *Daily Mail* was there for their delectation. Chris, the more serious of the pair, claimed the news section, while Carrol preferred the feature columns with all the show-biz chat. With no pressing concerns to rush them and all the time in the world to do as they pleased, this, they agreed, was the perfect way to start the day.

Later that morning, Tanya Miller ('such a little treasure') arrived at Mary Powell's home. She had hardly started on her cleaning chores before Mary's friends, Agnes Morrison and Jane Douglas, turned up. The self-styled Three Miss Marples were ready to get their teeth into the latest murder mystery which had been shown on television the previous night.

Although she would never be so bold as join in their deliberations, Tanya now understood what the three mad old women were up to. Quietly getting on with her work, she was secretly scornful of their conclusions. Having come to terms with the idiomatic speech of her three mistresses, her gleeful conclusion was that this time, 'they were,' as they might have put it themselves, 'up a gum tree.'

By mid-morning, the usual suspects were gathered at the men's retreat in the Old Folly. Top of the agenda as usual was the sporting news, crucial moments in the previous night's game being hotly debated, chiefly by Jim Curtis and Andrew Scott, who were Spurs and Arsenal fans respectively, with radically different opinions. Over by the ornate fireplace, matters of pressing international concern were discussed in a more rational fashion by the resident Brains Trust, headed by "Professor" Alexander Sinclair and the erudite Noel Davidson, all of them convinced that the government's fortunes would be immeasurably improved if only it heeded their advice.

One noticeable absentee from the regular group at the Old Folly was Dave Simpson. The somewhat dim Dave was otherwise engaged, having promised to accompany his lady-friend, Wilma Greenhorn, to the funeral of her neighbour, Anna Fulton. Making up the small party of dutiful residents were the doleful Hector Wainwright and the wee woman whose name no-one could ever remember. The funeral, like all "departures" from the Grange, was a discreet affair. Careful not to upset the ageing residents with a reminder of their own mortality, the cortege left from one of the car-parks on the periphery.

Around the same time, in what had once been a grand drawing room, Moira Muirfield, who in another life would have excelled as a Mother Superior, presided over the otherwise informal meeting of the ladies' handicraft club. This is, in effect, just a talking shop, since often enough little of a practical nature is ever achieved. To put it more bluntly, it is simply a panel of avid gossipmongers getting their teeth into the latest goings-on at the Grange, the more salacious the better.

In the early afternoon, members of the Grange's thespian elite meet up in the former ballroom. Today marks the first run-through of Gavin Madison's latest masterpiece, *The Horns of a Quandary*. A not entirely original drama written by the great man himself, starring Gloria Goodwood, the diva of the Grange. In it, Gloria plays a glamorous young woman who, believing her husband to have been killed in the war, marries again, only to discover when her first husband reappears that he had only been a prisoner of war. Derivative it may be, but you can be sure it will play to packed houses at every performance. Who needs Broadway or Shaftsbury Avenue when they have the Somerville Players on their doorstep?

Elsewhere, Grangers stroll carelessly around the lake, careful not to make eye contact with the model boat enthusiasts. In the walled garden, Ben Wilson and Eileen Grey, old flames who'd been reunited at the Grange, stop to chat with Alice Nolan and David Young, who'd been united by a bossy waitress.

Just another day at Somerville Grange, but not just any other day. Conscious that we may outstay our welcome, this will be our last visit. So tonight, when the shadows lengthen across the immaculate lawns, albeit reluctantly, we'll bid a fond farewell to the residents who've become our friends and leave them to see out their days in blissful contentment. Fortunate residents of the earthly paradise that is Somerville Grange.

Donald Montgomery (1940 – 20??)

Dear reader,

We hope you enjoyed reading *Welcome to Somerville Grange* Please take a moment to leave a review, even if it's a short one. Your opinion is important to us.

Discover more books by Donald Montgomery at https://www.nextchapter.pub/authors/donald-montgomery

Want to know when one of our books is free or discounted? Join the newsletter at http://eepurl.com/bqqB3H

Best regards,

Donald Montgomery and the Next Chapter Team

Printed in Great Britain
by Amazon